Years before, Valentine and the rest of his bear sleuth were captured, tortured, and bespelled by a circle of witches. Even after getting rescued, he still struggles with the aftereffects, and not just because the spells were reinforced with blood magick—demon blood, making them exceptionally difficult to counter. Finally, the Horseman of Death appears with the answer.

While the removal of the spells is nearly as agonizing and exhausting as having them placed on them in the first place, the sleuth still decides to go for a celebratory run. In his sluggishness, Valentine gets distracted by an enticing aroma and doesn't move fast enough, getting struck by a logging truck. As he struggles to get away on three limbs, the driver exits the truck, and Valentine is hit by the realization that the human is his mate—Stone, according to the name on his shirt.

Even with a newly broken arm, Valentine realizes he just may be having the best and worst day of his life. He's just met his mate . . . if he can find Stone, that is.

Logging for a Bear
Copyright © 2024 Charlie Richards
ISBN: 978-1-4874-3505-9
Cover art by Martine Jardin

Published by eXtasy Books Inc

Look for us online at:
www.eXtasybooks.com

Logging for a Bear
Kontra's Menagerie 38

By

Charlie Richards

DEDICATION

Change is the only constant in life. Ones ability to adapt to those changes will determine your success in life.

~Benjamin Franklin

CHAPTER ONE

"Hey, Congo. Do you and your guys have a minute?" Lifting his attention from the playing cards in his hand, Valentine turned halfway around to focus on the speaker. Beta Sam stood in the doorway, one shoulder leaning against the frame. The large Texas longhorn shifter had one hand shoved into the pocket of his jeans, and he was trying to appear relaxed as he eyed them all.

Except, Valentine noticed the lines of tension around the big shifter's firm mouth. Sam wasn't relaxed at all. For an instant, Valentine wondered what could be bothering him, but when Congo started rising while nodding, he figured he would find out soon enough.

"Sure, Sam." Congo tossed his cards face down on the table. "What's going on?"

Valentine copied his alpha's movements and rose to stand beside his cousin. The other pair—fellow bear shifters, Eurik and Zion—rose as well, also following their alpha's lead.

Seems our card game is over for now.

That was fine by Valentine. He'd been having a sucky game, anyway.

I should know by now, never play poker with Eurik when I'm having trouble focusing.

The other shifter was a card shark.

"Death is here, Congo," Sam told them, glancing around at them all. "He's talking to Kontra. Death says he has news."

Valentine knew the beta was referring to one of the Four Horsemen of the Apocalypse. They'd met all of them when

1

they were still under the control of a circle of witches who'd bespelled them to use for their own often evil and always selfish purposes. The Four Horsemen had destroyed the circle of witches, but that hadn't freed the bears from the influence of their spells—namely, obey the commands of certain people, especially magick-wielders. The order of a powerful warlock had tempered their lack of control, allowing them to live mostly normal lives, even if they were under the watchful eye of Alpha Kontra and his people.

"Do you need everyone?" Congo asked, moving toward Sam, who straightened from his lean. "Or just us?" Congo indicated the four of them who'd been playing cards.

Sam took a step backward. "All of you is probably best."

Zion headed toward the hall to the left. "I'll get the others," he stated as he strode off.

The others were the remaining members of their small sleuth—Congo's mate, Zhaul, as well as fellow bear shifters Madagascar and Shannon, plus their mates—Ishmael and Evan, respectively.

"We'll be in the study at the main house," Sam told him, and Zion waved in acknowledgment.

Their small bear sleuth was residing in a big A-frame that had been built behind a large farmhouse some years before. Evidently, a mated shifter and his human had needed their own space. The human's infant son needed quiet for nap time, and the rest of the flock-mates had a propensity for being quite loud.

That flock had moved on a couple of years before when one of their members had found his mate in Georgia.

As Valentine fell into step, flanking Congo, who was following after Sam, he did his best to ignore the jealousy mixed with sadness he felt as he thought about the other members of the sleuth—both alive and dead. His fellow bear shifters deserved their happiness after everything they'd endured, even as he wished for his own mate. On the other hand, those sleuth members that they'd lost before being rescued would never find the joy of their mates.

And for what? To line sadistic witches' pockets? Good riddance to those bitches. At least my sleuth-brothers are no longer in pain, either. Gods, I'm being maudlin tonight. Must be why I'm sucking at poker this evening.

Pushing those thoughts away, Valentine returned his focus to the goings-on. As they crossed the yard and moved through the great room of the farmhouse, he noticed that few of the shifters that made up Kontra's gang were around. Of course, seeing as it was a beautiful Tuesday afternoon in early spring, that wasn't surprising. It was the perfect day for a motorcycle ride through the mountains.

It would have been a great day to go for a run in bear form, too, but Shannon hadn't wanted to leave Evan. His warlock-in-training mate had had a rough day. Several of the spells he'd tried to cast hadn't turned out quite the way they should have, the last one of them leaving one of his mentors — Draven, a vampire warlock — with singed hair.

Valentine fought back a smile as he thought of how Draven had looked like a chia pet on one side, the left side of his head frizzy and poofy. Fortunately, Zhaul used to own his own salon. Congo's giant panda shifter mate had been able to give the vampire a very attractive style with his sides buzzed and his pale-blond hair a bit longer on top. It accentuated the man's lean, aristocratic features and made his blue eyes pop.

Not that I'm noticing the looks of other people's mates.

Ugh. I so need to get laid.

Sam stopped and knocked on a closed door, which led to the study.

Even through the door, Valentine heard the grizzly alpha's order for them to come in. He grimaced as he felt tingles along his spine, and the hairs on his arms and nape stood on end. Wincing, he exchanged a look with Congo, who quickly

3

pushed past a surprised-looking Sam. After opening the door, Congo rested a hand on Valentine's back and urged him into the room.

Valentine acted on instinct—and training—and came to a stop in front of the desk in parade rest fashion.

Kontra snapped his head up from whatever he'd been staring at and peered at him. His eyes widened a little before he blew out a deep breath. A muscle in his jaw flexed as he shook his head.

"Damn it," Kontra muttered, his brows creasing into a small scowl. "I didn't mean that as an order." He turned his attention to the left and stated, "I hope you're right because I can't wait for when I don't have to worry about this sort of shit."

Kontra waved his hand toward Congo and Valentine, obviously indicating their reaction to his command to enter the room. His expression softened as he refocused on them. "Please relax as you see fit."

Immediately, the odd buzz-like sensation that felt as if it crawled under Valentine's skin ceased. He took a deep breath and allowed his shoulders to relax. A glance at Congo told Valentine that his alpha was shaking out his arms while heaving his own sigh.

"I'm quite certain that I've discovered the counterspell."

The melodious tenor came from Kontra's left, drawing Valentine's attention. He'd been so focused on obeying the grizzly alpha's command that he hadn't even noticed the horseman's presence. The tall, slender male in black robes leaned against the wall. He sported a small smile, his expression appearing kind—which Valentine found odd, considering this was the Horseman of Death.

Huh. Never judge a book by its cover.

"Counterspell?" Congo questioned, a note of excitement filling his voice. "Counterspell, as in, to undo the enchantment the witches carved into our skin?"

"Exactly," Death confirmed.

Hope flooded Valentine, and he exchanged a grin with Congo. "That's the best damn news I've heard in years," he gushed while executing a fist-pump.

"What's the best news?" Madagascar asked as the rest of their sleuth crowded into the study. The room really wasn't built to hold so many large men, and Eurik and Zion remained in the doorway, peering over other men's shoulders. Madagascar stopped beside Congo, his brother, with his arm securely around the waist of his even larger wolf shifter mate, Ishmael. He placed the forearm of his free hand on Congo's shoulder. "What's goin' on?"

Death held up his hand, asking for silence and stalling more questions all at the same time. "Yes, I believe I have figured out the spell that will remove what the witches cast on you." Considering the horseman continued to hold up his hand, even as Valentine could smell the excitement that everyone was beginning to feel, he wondered what the problem could be. "But as I'm a horseman and not of this realm, it isn't something I can perform," Death explained, causing unease to slither down Valentine's spine. He wasn't the only one to begin glancing at the others in his sleuth. Fortunately, Death continued, "Kontra has messaged Draven and Tim so I can confer with them. As they are warlocks and of this realm, they should be able to complete the incantation."

"That's great," Zhaul exclaimed, grinning widely as he cuddled up against Congo. Hope and love filled his dark eyes as he stared at his mate. "Right?"

"Yeah, baby," Congo agreed, returning his warm smile. "It *is* great."

"There is one other thing," Death stated, redrawing their attention. His expression had turned pensive. "If I'm reading the spell properly, the process will hurt you . . . badly."

"Of course, it will," Eurik muttered with a scoff. Then he

smirked. "No pain, no gain. Right, guys?"

Zion jerked a swift nod. "Damn, right." He crossed his thick arms over his wide chest. "I'm more than willing to endure anything to remove this damn bespellment."

"That a word?" Valentine teased, smirking at his friend. "Bespellment?"

"Sure is," Zion declared as a smile teased at the corners of his lips. "When are we doing this?"

"Like Death said," Kontra cut in. "Death wants to talk to Draven and Tim first." He focused on Evan. "You should probably listen in, just for educational purposes."

Evan nibbled his bottom lip, even as he nodded slowly. "As long as they don't expect me to participate," he mumbled. His cheeks took on a pinkish hue as he glanced around at the group. Focusing on the floor, Evan muttered, "I wouldn't want to, um, jeopardize any of you."

"Evan." Draven drew out the apprentice's name as he slipped between the bear shifters and into the room. "I told you. We all made mistakes when we first learned." The slender male touched Evan's shoulder reassuringly before heading toward the desk and the book that was laid out before Kontra. "I look forward to seeing what you've found, Death."

Kontra focused on Zhaul. "Zhaul, I figure it may be a good idea if all you bears sat down and discussed it together." Valentine had seen the alpha use the technique before—speak to Congo's mate so whatever he said didn't trigger their bespellment, forcing them to obey him. "I understand this is a really big decision." After a second, Kontra added, "Especially since it's probably experimental."

Death nodded once in confirmation.

Zhaul nodded once. "Yes, Alpha Kontra." He glanced around at everyone. "Um, let's maybe go somewhere, uh, else."

Congo turned, keeping his arm around Zhaul. "Back to the

A-frame, guys," he encouraged with a shooing motion of his hand.

Valentine followed the others out, but in his mind, there wasn't a damn thing to discuss. If there was even the slightest chance of Death's spell working, no matter the pain, he intended to let the warlocks try it on him.

Any chance is worth the risk.

*

In the end, Valentine's opinion was held by all of them. They all wanted the spell to be done on them, so the warlocks agreed to do it to all of them at once. They sat in a circle in the backyard, waiting, as Draven and Tim set up the ingredients they needed around them to complete the incantation.

Valentine did his best to hide his nerves, but considering the scents filling the clearing, he knew he wasn't the only one feeling them. Silently, he prayed to whatever gods cared to listen that the spell would work.

Death's thought that it would probably be painful was an understatement.

It was *excruciating*.

As the warlocks began chanting, fiery tendrils rippled across Valentine's back. Sweat immediately beaded on his brow. With each second that Draven and Tim continued to speak, the sensation intensified and spread, until Valentine felt as if his flesh was being flayed from his body.

Unable to help himself, Valentine dropped to his hands and knees, then flopped to his belly. His body convulsed, and he couldn't stop the scream that erupted from his throat, and he wasn't the only one. Valentine heard the roars of his fellow sleuth-members echoing around him.

For an instant, Valentine heard the warlocks' voices falter. He could see them glance between each other, uncertainty on their faces. The three mated shifters' men were huddled together, clutching each other in an attempt to comfort each other as they stared at them with expressions of horror.

"Keep going," Valentine rasped.

In the same instant, Zion growled, "Don't stop."

Congo ordered, "Finish it."

After the other three bears all nodded, Draven and Tim continued.

Valentine dug his fingers into the grass as shudders racked his body. He wanted to tear off his clothes, feeling certain they had to be on fire. His ears rang with the cries echoing through the forest.

As blissful darkness descended, an inane thought popped into Valentine's head.

It's a good thing we're way out in the middle of nowhere or someone would call the cops.

CHAPTER TWO

Percy Stonewall leaned a hip against his semi's fender with his arms crossed as he watched the massive log loader machine lift the thirty-six-foot logs onto his trailer. Keeping a sharp eye, he made certain the young idiot behind the controls placed the logs uniformly. There was nothing more dangerous than poorly placed logs shifting while in transit.

Seeing the freshly placed log spin into an undesirable angle against the one next to it, he nearly pushed away from the truck to say something. Fortunately, the site foreman stepped in first. The man spoke into his earpiece, catching the loader's attention, and helped the obvious newbie adjust the log.

Then the foreman—Gerry Burke—headed his way, his rueful smile barely seen due to his thickly whiskered face. "Don't worry, Stone," he said by way of greeting. "We're keepin' an eye on this young gun, but he's learning quickly."

Stone nodded once, slowly. He knew Gerry was aware of his real name—Percy—but no one called him that. In fact, if anyone tried, Stone either ignored the person or threatened to knock their teeth in—depending on the situation. Even his work shirt sported his name as Stone.

Only his mother had gotten away with calling him Percy, and she was long passed.

"I appreciate that, Gerry," Stone replied, returning his attention to the loading of his trailer. "We seem to have a new set of trainees every year."

Meaning, Stone always kept a sharp eye on whoever was loading his trailer because they seemed to get younger every year.

Not that I'm that old.

But Stone sure felt it sometimes.

Stone had done two tours in the Army, working as a mechanic in the motor pool. The skills sure came in handy when anything on his rig broke down. Bills to pay to fix anything on the big machine could stack up damn swiftly.

After his time in the military, Stone had returned stateside and taken up trucking. He'd done long-haul for a few years until his mother had become sick. Stone had rented a cabin near her, bought his own rig, and become a logger. When his mother had lost her battle to cancer, he'd appreciated the fond memories their time together had given him. He'd bought the cabin and stuck around.

"That we do," Gerry agreed affably, turning to stand next to Stone. He focused on the loading, too, placing his hands on his hips. "This life sure ain't for everyone, and they either figure it out damn quick or stick around for years." Casting a smirking glance Stone's way, Gerry told him, "Most discover that playing with giant machines isn't nearly as glamorous as they think."

Stone scoffed under his breath. "No, it's not." Although, he'd sure enjoyed working on the military vehicles.

"Nice haircut," Gerry commented, glancing at him and taking in Stone's short red hair. "Never seen you with short hair before."

"Summer's coming," Stone replied gruffly, suddenly feeling self-conscious about the short, slightly spiky style that the barber had talked him into. The guy had winked and told Stone that it accentuated his cheekbones and blue eyes. Stone had been too uncomfortable with the guy's obvious flirting to say no. To get Gerry to stop staring, Stone claimed the first thing to come to mind and gruffly muttered, "Long hair was getting hot."

In truth, Stone couldn't remember if he'd ever had his hair

so short after leaving the military. He wasn't a prideful man, and he'd never had trouble getting laid when the itch hit him. Having his hair long or short had never really mattered beyond how easy it was to deal with.

Gerry nodded once and returned his attention to where it should be—the loading operator. "Fair enough." After the loader shut off the machine—*must be his break time*—Gerry grunted and took a step forward. "Have a safe trip."

Just when Stone was about to say, "Thanks," an odd noise filtered through the suddenly quiet trees. The hairs on the back of his neck stood on end. Narrowing his eyes, Stone tipped his head and listened, trying to decide just what in the hell he was hearing.

"Shit," Gerry muttered, scowling. "What the hell is that?"

"It sounds like . . . screaming," Stone murmured, a chill working up his spine. "Like someone screaming bloody murder."

Stone slowly spun, wondering where the noise was coming from. His adrenaline began to spike as he searched for the source. Instinctively, he felt the need to help, to make the obvious suffering stop.

Except, then the noise stopped, leaving him in uneasy silence.

Gerry cleared his throat, startling Stone and drawing his attention. The foreman was rubbing the back of his neck, looking just as uneasy as Stone felt. The scuff of a boot on rock caused them both to jerk.

Laughing, the noise sounding self-conscious, Gerry stated, "Must have been a wild animal makin' a kill."

Stone nodded once, although he wasn't certain he agreed. "Sure."

After clearing his throat, Stone swept his gaze around the area again, but there was nothing to see but trees, logging equipment, and the crew. He saw the pensive expression on the young loader's face. Stone felt about the same, but his military training kept his stoic mask in place.

"Well, have a safe trip, Stone," Gerry told him with a wave. "See you day after tomorrow."

Stone nodded, leaving Gerry to deal with his worried-looking loader. Heading to his trailer, he went through the process of tying down his load. He slid the bar into the slot on the crank and tightened the chains.

Satisfied with them, Stone made his pre-trip inspection, checking tires, gauges, and fluids. All the while, he listened for any noise that wasn't normal. The fact that the loggers didn't restart their equipment told Stone that he wasn't the only one preoccupied with the odd screams they'd heard.

With a shake of his head, Stone climbed into the cab of his truck. He eased noise-canceling buds into his ears before firing up his rig and rolling down his windows to feel the cool air on his face. The low rumble and vibration worked through him like the feel of a familiar caress.

Stone smiled as he checked his gauges before easing his truck into gear and releasing the brake. With a shift of feet and hands, he began working through his gears, starting his truck moving. He rolled out of the loading lot and rumbled down the gravel road.

Glancing back and forth, Stone kept an eye on the trees around him. He saw nothing but pines as he drove for several long minutes. Stone began to relax and reached over to grab his bottle of water.

Just as Stone twisted the cap off the bottle, several somethings darted from amidst the trees about thirty feet ahead of him.

"Shit," Stone hissed as he hit the brakes. The plastic bottle crunched as he instinctively tightened his grip. "What the—"

Stone realized he was seeing not one, but several large brown bears running across the road.

And is that a freakin' panda?

"What the hell?" Stone repeated, slowing, working to a stop as he drew closer to the weird sight.

As Stone watched the panda disappear between the pines, he felt his truck jolt. He snapped his focus in the other direction in time to see another bear spin around and, on three legs — his left foreleg held off the ground — lope back into the trees.

"Ah, damn," Stone muttered. "I just hit a freakin' bear." Placing his semi in park, he put on the brake before shutting down his rig. Staring into the trees on either side of the road, Stone didn't see any hint of the bears. "Hope I didn't hurt him too bad."

Stone enjoyed hunting every year, and one of the worst things to do was injure an animal without actually taking it out. There was no telling how much pain it could be in or where or when it would die from its injuries. Stone sure didn't want that for a bear he'd accidentally hit.

Reaching into his glove box, Stone pulled out his pistol. He opened his door and carefully climbed to the ground. Stone kept a sharp eye on the woods around him, listening for any sounds.

Stone heard nothing. Even the birds had ceased chirping. *Never a good sign.*

The hairs on Stone's neck lifted as he moved to the front of his truck. He took a quick glance at his front end. Stone noticed a slight dent, as well as scratches, but it was all very superficial.

Noticing some dark hairs caught between two panels, Stone reached out and plucked a few of them. He eyed them for a few seconds, rolling them between his fingers. They were several inches long and smoother than he would have assumed a bear's hair would be.

After another long look around, Stone let them fall to the ground. He blew out a long, slow breath as he squinted, doing his best to peer between the trees. Stone rubbed the back of his neck, still feeling as if he was being watched.

Stone shook his head as he tapped his *Glock* against his thigh, agitation plaguing him.

Knowing just how bad an idea trying to track the bear was, Stone turned away and returned to his semi's cab. He restarted his truck and continued on his way. After all, he had a load of logs to deliver.

Too bad Stone couldn't leave his worry and concern behind as easily.

Chapter Three

Pausing a few feet within the tree line, knowing he was out of sight, Valentine eased onto his butt. He cradled his left foreleg to his chest, pain radiating through the limb and into his body. Even with the ripples of agony pulsing through him, Valentine couldn't believe what had just happened . . . and it wasn't because he'd just been hit by a logging semi.

The scent that was wafting through the trees called to Valentine on a visceral level. His bear desperately wanted to go back to search for the source. Even his mouth salivated with a desire to taste the owner of that scent.

There could be only one reason for that.

My mate's here.

Peering through the trees, Valentine watched as a red-headed man paused in front of the semi. He glanced at the damage and plucked what Valentine assumed were a few of his hairs from where they must have been pinched when he'd been hit. Valentine noticed that the man kept most of his attention on the forest around him.

Valentine also noticed the gun in the man's hand.

He's understandably wary, considering he must have seen a sleuth of bears cross the road and he hit one of them.

Staying put was one of the toughest things Valentine had ever done. Every fiber of his being screamed at him to go confront the human. Except, Valentine knew he couldn't do it as a bear.

I should shift.

With that thought in mind, Valentine reached for his human form. He'd just started the change when he heard the sound of the semi firing back up. Even knowing it was probably too late, he pushed to become human even faster, pain from his limb shooting through him.

A low growl sounded in Valentine's ear, and Valentine recognized it as his cousin. Ignoring him, he continued to reach for his human form, his change slower than normal due to the damage to his limb. As soon as Valentine attained his bipedal state, he began pushing to his feet.

Hands grabbed Valentine, forcing him to stay on the ground. Snarling, he glared at Congo. His cousin just frowned back, shaking his head. Acting on instinct, Valentine ducked his head in submission to the shifter who was his alpha.

"What the hell are you doing, Val?" Congo demanded softly. "You just got hit by a freakin' semi."

"I smelled my mate," Valentine blurted swiftly, looking in the direction of the road. "Someone in that semi is my mate."

"Really?" Eurik appeared at his side, having also shifted. Kneeling beside him, he had a definite look of disbelief on his face. "How do you know?"

"First, when I entered the roadway, a smell teased me, distracting me," Valentine did his best to explain. "That's why I think I got hit. I heard the truck, but I was too busy trying to figure out where the smell was coming from to look for it." Frowning in the direction of the road once more, Valentine muttered, "Then there was the pain, and I knew I had to get away, but I couldn't make myself go far." Concern flooded Valentine, and he rubbed the back of his neck with the hand of his good arm. "I-I saw that hot redhead get out."

Even as a bear, Valentine had liked the way the human looked—broad shoulders that he wanted to nuzzle, a muscular neck he wanted to lick and bite, and short red hair he wanted to sniff.

Valentine's human brain had a few different ideas. He wanted to thread his fingers through those short, spiky red strands and check to see if they were soft or stiff with product. While Valentine had never given it much thought before, he wondered what kind of truck driver worried about style like that.

I'll find out before too long.

"What's going on, guys?" Zion asked as he crouched near them. The other shifter glanced between them all. His brows furrowed in obvious concern. "You okay, man? You're holding your arm."

"Val thinks his mate was in the truck," Eurik answered for him. "Anyone in there other than the driver who got out?"

Zion shook his head, his expression turning concerned. "No. I only smelled the one guy." After following Valentine's focus to the road, he stared at him again. "Um, he's gone." His troubled expression intensified as he looked toward Congo. "How the hell are we going to find him?"

"The man had a shirt on that read *Stone*," Zhaul pointed out. Congo's mate had also shifted to human form. He blushed a little as he added, "Uh, and with a haircut like that, I bet he had it professionally done. Are there any salons or barbers in Stone Ridge or the surrounding area?" When everyone glanced from the panda shifter, then at each other, Zhaul added, "We should ask Alpha Kontra or Alpha Declan and then ask about him there."

"Okay." Valentine's gaze strayed back to the road even though the sound of the truck engine was long gone. "Um, yeah."

Stone. What an awesome name for the muscular-looking male.

Valentine had noticed the guy's masculine frame and muscular arms. He would bet there were more muscles hidden under the human's dark-blue polo shirt. The way he filled it out had been a dead giveaway.

I want to see all that.

Anticipation caused his blood to heat and flow south.

Scoffing, Eurik grumbled, "None of whatever you're thinkin'." He rolled his eyes. "You're naked. Remember?"

Fighting back a blush, Valentine claimed, "At least the sensation of arousal beats out the pain in my arm." He sighed as he finally focused on his damaged limb. "Truck fender must have gotten me just right. I think it's broken."

That caught everyone's attention, and they all seemed to snap their attention to his left arm. Several of his buddies looked worried. A couple appeared troubled. Madagascar and Ishmael were still in bear and wolf form, but their concern was still evident by scent.

Congo growled, cuffing Valentine upside the head, albeit gently. "Gods damn it," he grumbled. "And you still shifted?"

Valentine curled his lip in a sneer. "Of course I did," he grumbled, even though he kept his eyes lowered. Congo was his alpha, after all. "He's my mate. I needed to try to meet him."

"Yeah, a naked man in the woods," Eurik teased, bumping his shoulder. "That'd certainly make a unique first impression."

Before Valentine could think up a reply—with his mate's scent having dissipated, he no longer had a distraction from the pain—Congo ordered, "Mads, will you and Ishmael run back to the cabin and see who's around?" He frowned as he added, "Maybe we can get a vehicle brought out here to get you, Val, so you won't have to walk all the way back."

Madagascar dipped his bear snout in a nod before turning and heading between trees and out of sight, his wolf shifter mate galloping after him.

"Hopefully, they'll be able to find us on this logging road," Eurik commented, rubbing the back of his neck. "How long do we wait?"

"They'll find us," Congo stated confidently, a smirk teasing at the corners of his lips. "The local wolf pack is run by park rangers. They'll sniff us out easy."

Several other men chuckled, as Valentine smiled vacantly.

"Congrats, man," Eurik murmured, patting him lightly on the back. "I'm damn happy for you." With a wink, he added, "And a little jealous. That truck driver was a hottie."

Valentine growled at his fellow bear shifter. "Eyes off. He's mine."

Lifting his hands in placation, Eurik grinned at him. "I know, man. I know." He laughed at him as he told him, "If you weren't injured, I'd smack you upside the head. Shifters don't poach."

"I know. Sorry," Valentine muttered with a deep sigh. "The ache in my arm is getting to me."

Not to mention the fact that he'd seen and scented his mate, but now the human was long gone.

Somehow, I'll find him, even if I have to stake out these logging roads.

"I wish we had a medic in our sleuth," Zion muttered, settling his bare ass on the ground. Resting his forearms over his knees, he stated wryly, "But if any of us were to examine you, we'd probably do more harm than good."

Their medic had been a man named Solomon. The bear shifter hadn't even made it through the attack when the witches had captured them. For a long time, Valentine had thought that had made him one of the lucky ones.

But now Fate is rewarding us for all our torment.

Valentine just had to believe the tales that his friends' spirits were reincarnated, and they would find their mates next time around.

"It's bearable," Valentine claimed, even though he was damn glad he was sitting down. He could already see that his forearm was beginning to swell. "I'll be fine."

Bumping his shoulder into Valentine's, Zion winked and asked, "Are you sure it's not *bear*-able?"

Valentine snorted and rolled his eyes. "Very funny."

Shifting to the left, Valentine leaned his back against a tree. He tipped his back against the trunk and did his best to ignore the pain as he listened to his sleuth-members chat.

*

Stepping out of the SUV, Valentine glanced up and down the street. He took in the sight of the small town, enjoying the quiet feel of it. Considering their sleuth had still been under spells when they'd first passed through Stone Ridge, they hadn't ventured into town. Valentine liked the look and feel of the place.

"You coming?" Congo asked, touching Valentine's upper arm.

Valentine turned his attention to his fellow shifter and nodded.

After giving him a smile, Congo slung his arm around Zhaul's waist and started down the sidewalk.

Looking through the window, Valentine saw the traditional chairs and sinks one would expect to find in a salon. There was a young man smiling and chatting as he cut a woman's hair. He sported eyeliner and a stylish hairdo.

A sudden surge of jealousy flooded Valentine at the thought that the young pretty human could have had his hands in Stone's hair.

"Hey, you okay?" Zhaul asked quietly, sounding concerned. "You're growling."

Rubbing at the cast on his left forearm, Valentine managed to cut off the sound. "Just dumb thoughts," he muttered with a scoff. "Uh, let's go."

Zhaul still looked worried for a second, but Congo had already opened the door to the salon. He was looking back at them with one black brow arched. Congo glanced back and forth at them, appearing questioning.

Valentine shoved his jealousy down deep and offered his cousin a wry smile. "Nerves, I guess."

"How's the arm?" Congo asked, holding the door open for him. "Feeling okay?"

Nodding, Valentine headed through the open door. "Lark's meds have done the trick," he told him.

Their group in the woods had been picked up by Alpha Declan and his human doctor mate, Lark. Several of their wolf shifters had been running beside the SUV, tracking for them. Evidently, Madagascar and Ishmael had noticed a logging road letter sign on their run back, giving the wolf shifter alpha a pretty good idea of where they'd been.

They'd taken Valentine—along with Congo and Eurik—back to their lodge-like home. The rest had run back to the large A-frame they were staying in, which had been built behind the big farmhouse that Kontra's people were staying in. At the lodge, Lark had the ability to X-ray, set, and cast his arm, and Valentine had learned that his arm had suffered a break in his radius. Fortunately, with his shifter healing, he'd only have to suffer through the indignity of the cast for a week or so. The doc had also supplied meds that worked on shifters, which was a very nice change.

"Glad to hear it," Congo told him with a pat to his shoulder while releasing the door. "Let's see what we can find out."

"Good afternoon, guys," the man who was styling the woman's hair greeted. "I'll be with you in just a sec." Offering them a wide smile, he added, "My receptionist just stepped out for lunch."

"No worries," Zhaul replied with a smile. "We have time."

Valentine wondered if the guy would be disappointed when they weren't really going to give him any business.

"Hi, handsomes," the man greeted as he headed over to

them a few minutes later. Looking over them with a speculative gleam in his eyes, he smiled widely. "Can't say I think you're here for haircuts."

"Afraid we're not," Zhaul confirmed with a smile that appeared apologetic. "I'm looking for a friend. His name is Stone." Lying through his teeth, Zhaul told him, "I was supposed to call him when I arrived in town, but my phone was damaged, and I've lost his number." With a wide smile, Zhaul laid it on thick and told the guy, "Stone sent me a picture of himself with his new haircut, telling me how much he liked it. Seeing your place, I was wondering if you gave it to him?"

"Oh, yeah. Stone?" The stylist began to gush, obviously appreciating the compliment. "He'd totally been hiding his hotness under his long hair."

Hearing the guy talk about his mate, Valentine kept his mouth shut. Fortunately, with Zhaul's fast-talking, he was able to sweet talk the stylist, getting him to look up Stone's number from his records.

Totally unethical, but whatever works.

Zhaul sent Stone's number to Lamar to look into, and anticipation filled Valentine.

Then how will I wrangle a meeting?

CHAPTER FOUR

Stone thanked the woman behind the counter for his coffee as he picked up the paper sack holding his bear claw. Turning, he headed toward the door of *Miss Martha's Muffins*. With his mind drifting back to the bears he'd seen—and the one he'd hit—three days before, Stone wasn't watching as he pushed the door open.

The door frame came to a jarring halt as it collided with someone who'd been walking by on the sidewalk outside.

"Damn it," the guy grunted, a noise of obvious pain.

While Stone didn't think he could have hit him that hard, a quick once-over of the man betrayed what had probably happened. The broad-shouldered black man had a cast on his left forearm. His dark brows were furrowed, and a grimace twisted his thick lips.

Realizing the door must have hit the guy's casted limb, Stone winced. "Ah, hell. Sorry about that, man."

Stone glanced at the couple of guys accompanying the man he'd hit, and worry slithered through his gut. They were both big, dark men—over six feet and built like linebackers. If they took offense at his mistake, he hoped they didn't try to kick his ass.

Then Stone felt a little bad about making that assumption, especially when the injured man smiled widely at him and offered, "No worries, man." Holding up his injured arm just a little, he added, "Funny how knocking the damn thing hurts more than when it originally happened." With a shrug, he continued, "Probably just the shock factor."

Stone nodded, surprised to find the guy's deep voice and friendly demeanor pleasing. No one who knew him would ever call him a people person. Even while in the military, Stone kept nearly everyone at a distance. He could count his real friends on one hand.

Except the guy before him, with the warmth filling his deep brown eyes, made Stone think of barbeques and relaxing with a beer together, shooting the shit. He could also see plenty of muscles hidden by the polo shirt the man wore. His calves bulged with definition, and the jean shorts did little to hide his thick thighs. Stone wondered what the man's body would look like nude, maybe oiled up like a bodybuilder's.

Such weird thoughts.

Hearing the coffee shop door's bell ring behind him, Stone moved out of the way of the exiting patron. "Well, uh, sorry again," he stated awkwardly. Indicating with his paper coffee cup, he added, "Hope that heals soon."

Beginning to turn away, Stone wondered at his reaction to the stranger. He couldn't remember the last time he'd wanted to linger in someone's company, leastwise a stranger and a man. Plus, the warmth in his gut unsettled him.

Am I feeling attraction for him?

Stone had accepted blowjobs from guys while in the military. Something about a man in uniform seemed to appeal to certain types of people, and a mouth was a mouth. He'd never thought that made him gay, though, or even bisexual. Stone had never returned the favor, and he'd certainly never wondered what a guy looked like naked or felt like to touch.

Good grief. What the hell's wrong with me?

"Oh, hey." The man gripped Stone's upper arm in a loose hold. "Just a sec. You're Percy, right? Percy Stonewall, but you go by Stone?"

Wariness slammed into Stone. The feel of the man's calloused hand on his arm caused the hairs there to stand on end. Heat radiated from that touch, making his stomach clench oddly.

Narrowing his eyes, Stone peered up to meet the taller, larger man's gaze. "Yeah. I'm Stone." He was damn sure he'd never met this man before, so he didn't ask an inane question like that. Instead, Stone said, "You've obviously asked around about me. You need something?"

As Stone spoke, he twisted his arm slowly, pulling free of the stranger's grasp.

The guy didn't appear offended by Stone's words or actions. Instead, he grinned. "Yeah, I do need something."

Of course he does.

"What?"

As a semi owner, Stone had had people ask for all sorts of things—from him hauling a car for them to letting them borrow his rig for something. He never allowed anyone else to drive his semi, but he didn't mind transporting other people's shit . . . for the right price.

"I'm Valentine," the man claimed, holding out his right hand to shake. "And I'd really like to take you on a date."

Stone grabbed his paper sack with the hand holding his coffee and took the man's hand on instinct, but upon hearing his request, he froze. Narrowing his eyes, he tipped his head a little. He needed to roll those words over in his mind several times before they made sense.

"I'm sorry," Stone began, confused as hell. "Are you asking me on a date?"

The man—Valentine—nodded, still giving him that wide, megawatt smile. "I am. Are you free for dinner this evening?" Before Stone could reply, he continued, "Or do you like to hike? This spring weather sure is nice, and we could check out one of the hiking trails around here." Valentine didn't give Stone a chance to say anything. Instead, he kept right on talking. "I'm new around here, so if you have a favorite, I'd be game to see it. I could pick you up at four."

Completely blown away, Stone found himself stuttering,

"O-Okay."

"Great!" Valentine grinned and squeezed Stone's hand, re-minding him that he'd never pulled away after the hand-shake. While rubbing his thumb over the back of Stone's hand, causing tingles to work up his arm, Valentine stated, "I'll pick you up at four then."

Then, to Stone's great shock, Valentine leaned down the couple of inches and bussed his lips over his temple, kissing him right there in the street. Finally, after giving him another huge smile, Valentine released him and turned.

As Stone watched Valentine and his two friends walk away from him, his brain felt as if it was misfiring because he couldn't resist checking out the big man's surprisingly tight-looking ass.

The honk of a horn in the street jolted Stone out of his stu-por.

Stone blinked once, twice, then turned to walk in the other direction, all the while wondering what the hell had just hap-pened.

Did I just agree to a date with a dude?

*

Stone kept his body and mind busy by completing a num-ber of domestic chores he'd been putting off — picking up gro-ceries, cleaning his small cabin, and doing laundry. It didn't completely work, but it was stuff he needed done anyway.

He'd been putting some of it off for a while because the last thing he wanted to do after driving a big loaded logging truck through windy mountain roads was to clean. Most evenings, after a long day behind the wheel, he blew off some steam on his workout equipment, did some stretching, then vegged in front of the boob tube with a meal and a beer.

While Stone would never consider himself a master chef, his mother had made certain he could feed himself.

"Can't have you starving until you find yourself a good woman to take care of you," she used to say. Then she would wave a wooden spoon at him and add, *"And that Army food is crap, and we both know it."*

So, a couple of times a week, Stone made a large casserole or slow cooker stew or something that could be divided into several days' worth of meals. He also had a kickass grill on his back patio. There was something so very soothing about enjoying a freshly cooked steak and baked potato amidst the beauty of nature.

"What would Mom think of me going out with a guy?" Stone muttered as he scrubbed the bathroom toilet. "What the hell was I thinking?"

Truth was, Stone knew he hadn't been thinking. As his mother would say, he'd been flabbergasted. Hearing Valentine's request, Stone hadn't known what to think or say.

Completing his task, Stone rose to his feet and began putting away his supplies. "I'll just have to set him straight when he gets here."

Stone certainly didn't want to lead the big guy on. That would be a dick move. Even though Stone didn't consider himself the nicest guy around — he had too many selfish, loner tendencies for that — he wasn't an asshole.

As Stone dried his hands and started for the shower, another thought struck him. "I didn't give him my address," he mused. "How the hell does he expect to pick me up? And he doesn't even have my phone number to call me and ask." Slowly, Stone peeled his dirty clothes from his body, tossing them into his laundry basket. "There's something really hinky about all of this."

Figuring time would answer his questions, Stone headed into the shower and scrubbed up. He kept it short and utilitarian. After rubbing himself down with a towel, he padded nude into his bedroom.

Stone stared into his closet, then rolled his eyes. "Not a

date. Not a woman," he reminded himself and turned to his dresser.

After slipping on a pair of briefs, Stone grabbed a pair of older, comfortable jeans. He chose a t-shirt and pulled a long-sleeved flannel over it, leaving it unbuttoned. Socks and hiking boots finished his outfit.

Then Stone went to his safe and opened it. He took out the ankle holster and pistol. Kneeling, he strapped it to his leg and positioned his jeans over it.

I don't know this man. Never can be too careful.

Seeing he had a good ten minutes before Valentine was supposed to arrive, Stone headed to his kitchen. He grabbed a bottle of iced tea and headed to his front deck. After settling on the porch swing, Stone rested one foot on the railing and started himself moving.

Stone popped the cap off his tea and settled in to wait while enjoying the warm late afternoon weather. He'd made it half-way through his tea when the sound of a throaty engine teased his ears. Cocking his head, he listened and waited, getting the impression that more than one vehicle approached.

A few seconds later, Stone's suspicions were confirmed. Three motorcycles appeared around a curve in the road and began slowing. The first bike — what appeared to be an older model, comfortable-looking *Honda Goldwing* — was driven by Valentine. The other two men from earlier drove the motorcycles flanking him.

Stone would be embarrassed if anyone pointed out that he was staring. Except, he was. He couldn't seem to yank his attention away from the big man driving the powerful machine. The guy wore a black half-helmet, a black leather jacket, and dark-blue jeans. It really wasn't anything special. When Valentine began slowing the machine and spotted him on the porch, he grinned broadly.

Stone felt the look like a sucker-punch to the gut, and his pulse kicked up.

Gee-zus.

Giving himself a mental smack upside the head, Stone rose to his feet. He set his tea on the railing and eyed the trio. Silence took over as all three turned off their machines.

"Hi, Stone," Valentine greeted, swinging off the *Goldwing*, the move accentuating his long, thickly muscled legs. "Hope you're having a good day."

"Was my day off, so . . . cleaning and other chores," Stone replied. As Valentine started toward him, a big smile on his face, he knew he had to set the guy straight. "Look, man, I think maybe you got the wrong idea about me." Stone lifted a hand, palm out in placation. "I've nothing against two guys together or whatever. What people do in their relationships is their own thing, but I'm not gay." Seeing Valentine pause at the bottom of the two steps that led to the ground and cock his head as he looked up at him, Stone quickly added, "Hell, I don't even consider myself bisexual. Never been attracted to a guy before."

Valentine shrugged and grinned before bounding up the steps to stand before him. "Until now, you mean."

Confused, Stone blurted, "What?"

Taking Stone's lifted hand in his good one, Valentine stated, "You said you'd never been attracted to a guy before. Until now." He squeezed Stone's palm before using his thumb to massage it, causing tingles of awareness to trickle up his arm. "You've never been attracted to a guy before now." With a roguish wink, Valentine claimed brazenly, "Because I know you're attracted to me."

With his body reacting to Valentine's nearness and touch—albeit sluggishly and with confusion—Stone wasn't certain what to say to that . . . because it was true.

Except – "How do you know?"

CHAPTER FIVE

Valentine knew Stone felt a combination of confusion, uncertainty, and even disbelief . . . the scents all mixed in with the heady aroma of his arousal.

My poor mate. He's telling me the truth, believing he's never been attracted to a guy. I'll have to try to be patient as I ease him into the idea of us.

Choosing his words carefully, Valentine stated, "It's the look in your eyes, Stone, and the way you respond to me." He didn't want to out and out lie to his mate, and telling him that he could smell his arousal was out of the question. With another squeeze to Stone's strong fingers, Valentine added, "You get a little tongue-tied around me and have trouble forming your thoughts." He wanted to thread the fingers of his other hand through his mate's short spiky red hair, but the cast made that impossible. Instead, he rubbed the pulse point on the inside of Stone's wrist. "You let me take your hand, and you haven't jerked it away, yet."

Stone's eyes widened, and his focus snapped to where Valentine still held him. Evidently, his human hadn't even realized their hands were still joined. Stone's brows furrowed, and he finally tugged on his hand.

Valentine immediately released him, not wanting to make him any more uncomfortable than he already did, even though he immediately missed the contact.

Deciding to move things along, Valentine pivoted and indicated his motorcycle. After agreeing to follow Kontra to

Stone Ridge, they'd all picked up used bikes. He found he enjoyed the freedom of zooming along, feeling the wind on his face.

"Are you ready to go?" Valentine asked. "I packed us a picnic dinner." Taking a step in that direction, he explained, "I know a couple of the park rangers, and they gave me a couple of ideas for short hikes that offer great views and places to stop and eat and relax."

One even had a swimming hole, and Valentine would love to talk his mate into skinny dipping with him.

Mmmm . . . Stone wet and naked.

Predictably, Valentine felt his blood flow south. Arousal surged through him, hot and fast. His dick plumped behind his fly, and he feared he would end up experiencing a rather uncomfortable ride and hike.

Stone's next words helped ease his ardor a bit.

"You expect me to ride bitch on your motorcycle?" Stone scoffed as he shook his head. "I don't think so."

Valentine hesitated, wondering how he could change his mate's mind. It hadn't even occurred to him that Stone would refuse. Many of the guys' mates were happy to ride with their partners.

Fortunately, Stone added, "Let me grab my motorcycle's keys and jacket." He started toward his front door. "Be right back."

After Stone disappeared inside, Valentine exchanged looks with his fellow bear shifters—Eurik and Zion. Congo had insisted that Valentine not go alone, considering he was riding a motorcycle in a cast. That and if, by some bizarre twist, paranormal explanations started, one of the two would be able to prove their ability to change into bears since Valentine couldn't in a cast.

"So, your man has a bike," Zion commented with an eyebrow waggle. "Fate knows her shit. Payson says motorcycle sex is awesome."

Valentine chuckled, nodding. He felt a wave of heat wash through him at just thinking about sex in relation to Stone. Hearing his mate's approaching footsteps, Valentine cleared his throat, turned to look at him . . . and nearly swallowed his tongue.

Stone in jeans, a flannel, and boots was sexy enough. Add in a black leather jacket and a helmet under his arm, and he was absolutely drool-worthy. The way the leather spanned his shoulders made Valentine want to reach out and explore.

Clenching his fingers to keep from doing just that caused a burst of pain in his healing arm. At least that helped him focus . . . as well as eased his arousal somewhat. He watched Stone lock his door, and he was helpless to stop himself from staring at his mate's jeans-clad ass.

Once again, the urge to touch flooded him, and he had to swallow a groan.

Stone turned and paused. He narrowed his eyes just a little, even as he arched one brow. His expression told Valentine that he'd totally been caught ogling the man's ass.

As if I care.

Valentine grinned widely, not even a little abashed. "You're sexy," he declared, giving Stone a sweeping, appreciative look. "Very, *very* sexy."

After a hard swallow, and Valentine didn't miss the slight pinking of the man's cheeks, Stone muttered, "Thanks."

"Come on, Stone," Valentine encouraged, moving down the couple of steps. "Let's get rolling."

Valentine assumed Stone's motorcycle was in a small garage since the semi could clearly be seen in a carport-type structure with half-open sides. When Stone opened the rolling door, his suspicions were confirmed, and he let out a whistle of admiration. Except, it wasn't his mate's bike that he found interesting because that was hidden under a cover. Instead, the place was clean and filled with a number of toolboxes lining some of the walls while a myriad of other tools hung on others. Storage shelves were filled with items such as jacks and things that Valentine couldn't hope to identify.

"Adam would love this place," Valentine murmured, taking it all in.

Stone pulled off the cover, revealing an older, vintage *Harley*. "Who's Adam?" he asked over his shoulder while folding the cover and placing it on a workbench.

"Adam is part of a motorcycle gang staying in the area for a little while," Valentine explained. "He's their group's mechanic." Scoffing, he peered around the small garage again. "Bet this place would give him a boner."

"Uhhhh, I really have no response to that," Stone muttered, settling his helmet on his head and buckling it. Frowning at him, he asked, "Is that a good thing?"

Valentine snorted. "Adam's partner Noah would probably think so."

Seeing Stone's lips part a little as he gaped at him in disbelief, he barely managed not to grab the human and lay one on him. Valentine wanted to taste his mate's mouth in the worst way. Perhaps Stone read something in his expression, for his brows shot up, and he took a step backward. The move jerked Valentine out of his lustful thoughts, and he cleared his throat and turned away.

"So, did you want to offer a suggestion on a destination?" Valentine asked, needing to focus on something other than his handsome human. "Or should I pick one that the rangers recommended?"

Gripping his motorcycle's handlebars, Stone righted the bike and began pushing it forward. "Depends on how long a hike you want and how hungry you all are, so you can pick." As he spoke, he moved his *Harley* out of the garage. Using his chin, Stone indicated the pull rope dangling from the top of the rolling door. "Can you get that for me? Just flip the lever, and it'll lock."

33

Valentine nodded and did as Stone requested. He turned just in time to see his mate swing a long, lean leg over his bike. His mouth watered at the magnificent sight of Stone getting ready to ride with him.

Maybe it won't be too long before he's riding me.

With a mental roll of his eyes, Valentine started back to his waiting friends. That was about the time he realized he hadn't introduced them. Valentine quickly remedied that, explaining that he and the pair had been friends for decades.

"Decades?" Stone questioned. "Since you were kids, huh?"

Realizing Stone was guessing his age to be in the thirties, Valentine knew he couldn't correct him. His mate wasn't ready to hear that Valentine was over a century old.

Instead, Valentine nodded. "Feels like it. We've been through a lot together." With a scoff, he added, "They wouldn't let me drive around the mountains by myself with this cast on." Valentine waved his arm before climbing onto his own bike.

"Damn straight," Zion claimed. "Safety first, man."

"Always a good motto," Stone agreed. Smirking, he pointed at Valentine's casted arm. "Sure you don't want to ride bitch to me?"

For a second, Valentine was ready to blurt out, *"Hell, yeah. I'd be happy to."* Then he noticed the twinkling in Stone's eyes, the teasing glint within his blue depths, and he realized his mate's offer wasn't actually sincere. Valentine liked that his human teased him, even if he felt a measure of disappointment, too. "If I thought your offer was even a little sincere, I would take you up on it in a heartbeat," Valentine declared, holding Stone's gaze. "I would love to wrap my arms around you and hold you as you drive us down the road." Seeing the way Stone's eyes widened as shock filled his gaze, Valentine softened his smile and added, "But I know you're not ready for that, handsome." Returning his helmet to his head, he ordered, "Fire up your engine, Stone. Let's get this date on the road."

Without waiting for a response, Valentine started his *Honda*. His friends followed his lead. He idled for a minute, waiting for Stone to do the same. Once his mate did, Valentine made a decision on where to go.

"Hey, Zion," Valentine called. "You wanna lead the way to the Old Lumbermill Trailhead?"

Zion gave him a *thumbs up*, then started them on their way.

Technically, where they were going wasn't an actual trailhead. Instead, it was a location Alpha Declan had shown him on the map. He'd explained that it had once been a lumbermill camp, but it had fell into disuse when laws had changed regarding logging in the area. A few of the old buildings still stood on the banks of the river, and there was a beautiful waterfall.

The place was popular with shifters, so if anything odd happened, it would also be a great segue into explaining the paranormal.

Valentine doubted that would come up so soon, but the overgrown, nearly hidden logging road was an easy hike. The final setting was a beautiful area. Plus, with the water, there was always a chance of swimming.

Yup. Can't beat that.

Making his way along the roads, Valentine occasionally glanced at Stone, who rode beside him. He admired the way the man expertly handled his bike. Valentine found his mate's confidence on the *Harley* sexy.

Okay. I find everything about my mate sexy.

Valentine smiled at that thought.

Just as it should be. Damn, Fate's been good to me.

CHAPTER SIX

Stone noticed the appreciative looks Valentine gave him as they drove through the windy mountain roads. As he drove, he tried to process them. He couldn't remember the last time anyone had looked at him like that—as if he was the best thing he'd ever seen.

As if I'm a steak, and Val hasn't eaten in weeks.

But he's a dude. Sure, I didn't mind a few sucking my dick, but that was different.

Considering Valentine had gone through the trouble of tracking him down and asking him on a date, Stone didn't think the man was interested in just a quick bump and grind before they both went their separate ways. A date in the woods was too romantic a gesture. It said, *let's get to know each other to see if we're compatible.*

Stone hadn't looked for anything beyond a quick pick-up in more years than he could count. Finding a permanent partner wasn't even a blip on his radar. He didn't know what to think about the sudden, unexpected attention.

While it made Stone uncomfortable, he didn't make a habit of lying to himself. He had to acknowledge that Valentine had been correct when he'd declared that Stone found him attractive. Stone didn't know why, but there was just something about him that seemed to check Stone's boxes in a way he'd never experienced with anyone.

The fact that it was a guy was definitely throwing him for a loop.

If he was a woman, would I be struggling this much? Or would

I be the one asking her on a date?

In truth, Stone really didn't know. His thoughts revolved back to the fact that he hadn't been looking for a relationship. Stone couldn't remember the last time he'd dated anyone.

High school, maybe?

It was sort of expected in order to get a date for the prom.

When Valentine's friends began slowing, Stone snapped his attention on where it should be—driving. He knew better than to allow his mind to drift while riding his motorcycle. That was a recipe for disaster.

Peering around the area, Stone followed the others off the road and onto a narrow, grass-covered track. He frowned, not entirely certain where they were. Stone had allowed his mind to drift too much while sorting through his thoughts and feelings.

Not that Stone had really gotten anything sorted, at all.

Everything about the situation was odd as hell.

The group continued along the narrow path—Stone wouldn't even call it a road—for another several hundred yards before it petered out. The guys turned their bikes around so they were facing out. Then they shut them off and relaxed on their kickstands.

Stone followed suit and dismounted when Valentine did. After removing his helmet, he locked it in a side bag, placing his leather jacket in there, too. He knew if they were hiking, he wouldn't need it.

While Valentine pulled out what was obviously a picnic basket and a blanket from his saddlebags, the other pair didn't even get off their bikes.

When the pair saw Stone looking at them, Zion smiled at him. "We're not crashing your date, man," he told him. He rested his forearms on the front of his bike and shrugged one large shoulder. "But Val's cousin, Congo, would kick our asses if we allowed him to wander around the mountain alone while he's injured."

"Yeah," Eurik added his two cents. "Congo's protective of all of us, but Val's family, after all."

Confused, Stone asked, "Why's Congo protective?"

Stone noticed Valentine had tucked his own helmet and jacket away and currently had a blanket draped over his shoulder.

Wow. He's going all out.

"Uhhh." Valentine looked like a deer caught in headlights, uncertain what to say or do.

Zion cleared his throat while Eurik rubbed the back of his neck.

Ooookay. They're obviously hiding something.

Unease slithered up his spine, and Stone felt the hairs on his nape stand on end.

Heaving a deep sigh, Zion rubbed a hand over his clean-shaven jaw. "Okay, look," he began, obviously coming to a decision. "I can't tell you everything. It's confidential." His black brows furrowed as a muscle ticked in his jaw. "What I can say is . . . we were in battle. We were captured. Some of the guys in our . . . troop . . . didn't make it." Something dark moved behind the big man's eyes, like a remembered pain. "Congo's not just Val's cousin, but our leader. So those of us that survived and were rescued, well, he feels a certain amount of responsibility."

"Even though there wasn't shit he could have done about it," Eurik cut in, his voice a rough growl. "Shit happens, man."

The fact that these men were ex-military made sense to Stone. Between their size and bearing, the way they watched their surroundings while watching out for each other, could all be explained by POWs returning with a healthy dose of PTSD. Hell, while Stone had never been diagnosed, he occasionally suffered his own bouts of insomnia and nightmares.

Lifting a hand to stop them from saying more—orders were orders, after all—Stone told them, "I get it. I was in the motor pool, so" — he waved his hand dismissively — "no need to try to explain more."

"Thanks for understanding, man," Zion replied with a smile.

Valentine appeared a little concerned, as if he wanted to say more.

Maybe realizing the same thing, Eurik clapped his hands together and stated, "Okay, guys. You have a great hike and date." He leered as he winked and teased, "Don't do anything I wouldn't do."

"Shoot us a text when you're on your way back out, Val," Zion ordered, leveling a serious look at him. "Or you'll never hear the end of it from Congo."

Valentine groaned as he rolled his eyes. "Yeah, yeah," he grumbled under his breath. With a shake of his head and a sigh, he mumbled, "You'd think I was five or something."

"It's or something, man," Zion called over the roar of his newly fired-up motorcycle.

With another wave, both men headed off.

Stone focused on Valentine and arched a brow. "So, uh, protective much now, huh?"

"Afraid so," Valentine admitted with a grimace. His black brows furrowed as he picked up the picnic basket. "Hope that doesn't make you think less of me."

Falling into step beside Valentine, Stone admitted, "Actually, I'm a little jealous." He took in the way the larger man's brows shot up, and he admitted, "I don't have any family. It was just my mom and me, and she passed a few years back."

"I'm sorry," Valentine rumbled, offering him a wry smile. "I can offer you my family, but you've just seen how protective we all are of each other." After issuing a low laugh and shaking his head, Valentine told him, "You may not like 'em when they meddle."

Stone nodded, taking that at face value. "I *am* a pretty private person. It's the reason I drive a semi," he admitted, glancing Valentine's way before refocusing on the woods and where he was putting his feet. "It's good money, and I don't have to deal with a bunch of idiots very often. Not sure I want a bunch of strangers suddenly all up in my business."

Reaching out, Valentine touched the backs of his casted fingers to his upper arm. "But they're a support system, too," he told him, appearing concerned. "If you ever need anything, they'll always have your back."

Uncertain how to respond to that, Stone kept his mouth shut. Looking around the woods, he changed the subject, instead. "This isn't a real trailhead," he pointed out. Stone glanced Valentine's way, arching his brow. "You said you know the park rangers around here. Did they tell you about this place?"

While Valentine gave him a knowing smile, he didn't call Stone on the blatant shift. "Yeah. The head ranger is Declan, and he's a friend of"—pausing, he waved his casted hand in dismissal—"it's a friend of a friend of a friend thing. When I said I wanted to take you on a hiking date, this was one of the places recommended." Pointing at the narrow path, Valentine told him, "As long as we don't stray, we'll get there in under thirty minutes, and it's supposed to be a really great place for a picnic, to relax, and even take a dip if we want."

"A dip?" Stone narrowed his eyes as he eyed Valentine. "As in swimming?"

Valentine grinned widely. "Yep." From his gaze sweeping over him, the guy's innuendo couldn't be missed when he asked, "Fancy a skinny dip, handsome?"

Stone groaned as he shook his head, doing his best to ignore the rush of heat the look and words caused. "That's the worst line, ever, man," he stated, instead. "You're really trying to get into my pants, aren't you?" Unable to help himself,

Stone asked, "Is that all this is? Are you horny, think I'm hot, and want to get me naked for a few hours of fun before we go our separate ways?"

On the way there, Stone would have sworn that wasn't the case, but he had to ask. For some reason, thinking about it, saying it, caused an uncomfortable twist in his gut. He did his best to ignore it, since he had no clue how to process the sensation.

Surely it's not disappointment.

"Not a chance," Valentine replied gruffly. There was even a slight growl in his voice. He cleared his throat before saying, "That's not what this is at all." After a second of hesitation, Valentine chuckled depreciatively before adding, "But I don't want to come on too strong and freak you out, either."

Why the hell do I feel relief?

"Oookay," Stone responded quietly. Rubbing the back of his neck, he wondered if he could get away with another subject change. "So, uh—"

He was coming up blank. That was another reason he didn't try to date. Other than trucks and work, he didn't really have a lot to talk about.

Spotting Valentine's cast, Stone asked, "So, uh, what happened to your arm, anyway?" He seemed to be using it fairly well, but the cast looked new.

"Got hit by a truck," Valentine revealed with a grimace. "Not my finest moment."

"Hit by a truck?" Stone froze for an instant, the image of the bear limping into the woods coming to mind. "Damn." He pushed his residual guilt away and jogged a couple of steps to catch up. "Sorry to hear that."

Valentine actually smiled at him. "Eh, like I said. Not my finest moment." With a roll of his eyes, he claimed, "Certainly wasn't the trucker's fault. I'm the idiot who got distracted while out running and strayed too far into a road without looking where I was going." Lifting his arm, Valentine told him, "I'm lucky this was the only injury I came away with, and it'll be healed in a couple of weeks."

"Happened a while ago, then, huh?" Stone thought that made sense with how easily Valentine was moving. "Glad to hear you're on the mend."

Stone had never broken anything, but he'd seen plenty of battle-buddies taken out by fractured limbs and torn ligaments. The body was a pretty fragile thing, but at least it was resilient. There was so much that they could heal from.

Except sometimes cancer.

With a small smile, Stone realized that his mother would probably have liked Valentine. While he didn't know what she would have thought of his pursuit of him, if they'd met each other in some other situation, she would've liked Valentine instantly. She would've loved his energy and relaxed nature.

Hell, I like that about him, too.

So many people would take just such a type of accident and tried to twist it to their own end. Too many people sued others instead of taking responsibility for themselves. Instead of blaming the driver of the vehicle, Valentine took it in stride and admitted his fault.

Stone found that commendable, raising Valentine's esteem in his eyes.

They walked in silence for several minutes, and Stone enjoyed the scent of pines and the sounds of animals scampering through the underbrush. The quiet between them was comfortable as opposed to oppressive. He didn't feel the need to fill it, and evidently, Valentine didn't either.

A few moments later, Stone recognized the sound of rushing water ahead. It wasn't long before a clearing opened before them. A number of rotting tree trunks littered the massive space, and dilapidated buildings were half-hidden in the encroaching forest.

Sweeping his gaze over the area, Stone took in the falling

structures and moss-covered walls. He squinted into the trees and made out the edges of five buildings—two sheds, a long building that could have been a barracks, and two huge structures that had probably held machines.

Stone had a strong desire to explore as he muttered, "This is impressive. I wonder how long ago this logging camp was abandoned."

The name of the trail Valentine had told Zion to lead them to now made sense—Old Lumbermill Trailhead.

Unable to help himself, Stone started between trees toward the nearest building.

CHAPTER SEVEN

For nearly thirty minutes, Valentine followed Stone through the crumbling remains of buildings. His mate was apparently fascinated with the weather-beaten and overgrown structural remains. Stone even spouted off a few facts about logging that had happened in the area in the past.

Well, what do ya know. My mate's a history nut.

Valentine thought that was damn endearing, considering he was a large, fit trucker.

Once Stone had explored to his heart's content, Valentine led the way to the lake's edge. The mist of the waterfall felt fantastic against his heated skin. Hanging around Stone had that effect on him.

After spreading out the blanket, with Stone's help when gripping it in his left hand proved awkward, Valentine sat on one corner and opened the basket. He spread the contents on the blanket. Valentine hadn't had a clue what his human would be interested in, so he'd brought an assortment of different things.

There were three types of finger sandwiches — turkey, roast beef, and egg salad. The fruit salad contained chunks of watermelon, cantaloupe, honeydew, kiwi, strawberries, green grapes, and slices of mandarin oranges. He'd included containers of potato salad, pasta salad, and French onion dip with chips. For drinks, he had a canteen of wine, a six-pack of beer, and several cans of soda, as well as bottles of water.

"How the hell did you fit all that in that basket?" Stone asked, staring at the assortment in surprise. As he settled across from Valentine, he shook his head. "It must have been heavy as hell. I wish you would have told me." Looking troubled, Stone told him, "I could at least have carried the blanket."

Valentine grinned at Stone. The fact that his mate worried about him warmed him from the inside out in a completely non-sexual way. He really liked it.

"It wasn't so heavy," Valentine reassured. As much as he liked that Stone was concerned about him, he didn't *actually* want to see him worried. It was just a nice sentiment. "Besides, the trail was easy, and the blanket was just resting on my shoulder. Not so hard to handle." Hoping to get Stone to focus on something else — namely, the food he'd provided — Valentine admitted, "I really had no idea what would interest you, so if you don't like something, don't feel obligated to eat it."

Stone relaxed, letting out a chuckle. "Don't worry. I won't." Smirking at him, he took the paper plate Valentine held out to him. "I don't do much that I don't want to, Val." Stone shrugged. "You'll figure that out sooner or later."

Valentine smiled back, inordinately pleased that Stone was making an innuendo that he would be around long enough for Valentine to learn things about him.

After placing plastic serving spoons in the different dishes, Valentine asked, "What would you like to drink?" He watched with pleasure as Stone began helping himself and told him of his drink options.

Stone's attention fell on the six-pack of beer, and he appeared to be reading the label. After a second, he nodded toward it. "I'm not familiar with that brand, but I'll give it a shot." With a chuckle, he added, "Worst case scenario, I won't like it, and I'll have a water."

"Not a soda?" Valentine asked. After easing a can out of the plastic ring, he popped the cap and held it out. "Like a different flavor?"

"Naw," Stone replied, taking the offered beverage. "Just not a soda fan. Too much sugar. Too much carbonation. Too sweet. There's a few that I like, but it's just not worth the hassle to buy them on the regular." After taking a swig and swallowing, Stone hummed as if he were analyzing the taste. "Not bad."

Evidently, he had been.

Recalling the bottle of iced tea Stone had placed on his porch railing, Valentine absently commented, "I'll keep the fridge stocked with tea, then."

Stone began to nod, then paused and tipped his head a little. Narrowing his eyes, he stared at him for a long moment.

Valentine could imagine what his mate was thinking— *that's a very couply thing to do . . . or that screamed of relationship . . . or—*

"I guess I'd appreciate that," Stone mused so softly that Valentine almost missed it. Then Stone cleared his throat and shoved a corner of a small roast beef sandwich into his mouth.

Okay. Headway.

I'll take it.

After taking a bite of a turkey sandwich, nearly biting the mini sandwich in half, Valentine chewed as he took in what food Stone had favored. He'd taken quite a bit of fruit salad, but he'd picked out the honeydew. While he'd taken a small amount of pasta salad, he'd taken much more of the potato salad, adding mustard to it from single-use packets Valentine had brought with the intention of using them on the sandwiches.

Interesting.

Every once in a while, Stone would reach into the chip bag and dip it into the French onion dip. He would pop it into his mouth and hum almost obscenely. If Valentine had to guess, Stone didn't eat the stuff often, even though he obviously enjoyed it . . . *a lot.*

Their conversation was relaxed and lowkey.

Valentine did his best to keep any sexual content out of it. He didn't want his mate to feel uncomfortable or pressured. Instead, Valentine was hoping that Stone would just get used to his company, to the idea of them hanging out together.

That didn't mean Valentine didn't occasionally take the opportunity to touch Stone. When he handed him a couple of napkins, he teased his fingertips against Stone's palm. While passing over another beer, Valentine slid his knuckles over Stone's. At one point, he couldn't resist leaning over with a napkin and wiping a dab of mustard from his lip.

Stone turned just the faintest hint of pink and turned his attention toward the water, so Valentine immediately found another banal subject.

"I'm going to guess from your fit body that you work out quite a bit," Valentine guessed, sweeping his gaze over him appreciatively. "I know the stereotype of truck drivers is fat, overweight, a bit unkempt." Seeing the way Stone's eyes widened, Valentine quickly added, "But you're none of those."

Barking a laugh, Stone grinned at him. "Yeah, there's a number of truckers who give us a bad name, but we're not all like that." Then he winced and shrugged. "Okay. A lot of them are. Maybe that's why I'm usually pretty mindful of what I eat and drink, and I have a weight set in my second bedroom that I use four or five times a week." Stone smiled as his expression turned a little vacant. "I also have some rope and obstacle courses set up in the forest behind my house. Great to loosen up sore muscles after long days in a bouncy truck seat."

"That's awesome, Stone," Valentine commented, meaning it. "I love the great outdoors, too." As a bear shifter, that was a given, but Stone didn't know that yet. "Never tried a rope course, and I don't know how agile I'd be with obstacles, but I wouldn't mind giving it a shot."

Stone stared at him for a long moment, as if judging Valentine's honesty. "Okay," he finally replied. Shifting in his seat, he asked, "So, uh, what about you? What do you do for fun?" Then he paused with another roast beef sandwich poised before his mouth. "How long have you lived around here?" Furrowing his brows, Stone asked, "Where did you see me that I didn't notice you?" As if realizing how that sounded, Stone quickly pointed at him. "I mean, you and your friends are sort of hard to miss."

Valentine grinned as he chuckled. "We are, that's for sure." He wasn't offended. Bear shifters were normally pretty big in human form. "And we like card games, and I don't just mean poker." Chuckling, Valentine shared, "We're a pretty competitive bunch, and we recently found a card game called *Dutch Blitz*. We bought the expansion pack so we can all play." Thinking of the yelling and hollering that often filled the house when they all stood around the table flipping cards as fast as they could, Valentine laughed. "Yeah, that can get rowdy."

"I don't know that one."

On instinct, when Valentine heard that admission, he told him, "I'll teach you. It's a lot of fun."

To his pleasure, Stone shrugged and nodded. "Okay."

For another few minutes, Valentine and Stone again focused mostly on eating. There were a few quiet hums of enjoyment and grunts of pleasure. After a bit, Stone leaned back on one hand and rubbed his belly with the other.

"That was really good, Val," Stone stated appreciatively. "Thank you."

"You're welcome." Valentine would have preened if it wouldn't have made him look ridiculous. "I'm glad you enjoyed it."

Stone looked over the offerings as he asked, "Did you really prepare all this yourself?"

Valentine chuckled while shaking his head. "Not a chance," he admitted. "I had a lot of help from the guys."

Cocking his head, Stone pointed out, "You and your friends refer to the guys and friends of friends quite a bit. Can you explain that a little?" He frowned. "Are you living with friends from the area or something after your, uh" — he hesitated a couple of seconds before finishing — "your ordeal."

Thinking about his *ordeal*, Valentine swallowed hard. That was one word for it. He knew he would have to explain it all to Stone eventually. Still, he knew that time was still a ways off.

Thank the gods.

That was going to be a painful conversation.

"Um, I'll try to explain a little," Valentine told him slowly, thinking quickly about how to do just that.

Valentine built on the premise that Kontra was the leader of his own platoon of men who'd turned into a biker gang, and they specialized in rehabilitating those traumatized by war. He explained how, after they were rescued, he and his buddies were put in Kontra's care. He left out any mention of the paranormal, not wanting to send his mate running for the hills.

"Damn, it's good that those guys were available to help you," Stone murmured with an expression of concern. He opened his mouth as if to ask something but snapped his jaw shut just as quickly.

"You can ask me anything, Stone," Valentine told him with a reassuring smile. "If I can't answer, I'll be honest about that, too."

Nodding, Stone still hesitated. After sweeping his gaze around the clearing, his attention fell on the large pool created by the waterfall. He frowned at it for a short while, and Valentine took a sip of his beer, letting him sort his thoughts.

Finally, Stone mused, "I really thought you would've tried to get me naked and in the water by now."

Valentine choked on his swallow of beer. Coughing hard, he managed to get control of himself before he sprayed it everywhere and made a complete ass of himself. As Valentine breathed through his nose, he took in Stone's amused expression.

"Sorry about that," Stone offered, although he didn't sound at all sincere.

"Ha, ha," Valentine muttered, frowning at him. Then he sobered and admitted, "If I thought there was a chance, I would have already asked, but I was trying to be a gentleman." Seeing Stone arch his brow in surprise and disbelief, Valentine added, "And I didn't want to pressure you. Even though I know you're attracted to me, I didn't want to send you running or somethin'."

Stone licked his lips. Sweeping his gaze over Valentine, he swallowed hard enough to cause his Adam's apple to bob. Finally, he nodded once.

"Yeah. Yeah, I find you attractive," Stone admitted, causing Valentine's heartrate to spike. "Never felt actual attraction to a guy even though I've gotten hard around them before."

It was Valentine's turn to pin Stone with a questioning look.

With a shrug, Stone didn't meet his gaze as he explained, "Went to clubs and shit while on leave. Been hit on by guys. Took advantage of their offers to suck me off."

Hearing about others touching their mate was never something a shifter wanted, but Valentine stayed his desire to growl possessively. Instead, he jerked a nod. "So." He couldn't help that his voice came out a little gruff. "You don't have an issue with getting a blowjob from a man?"

"No, I don't." Stone stared at him, a tick setting off in his jaw.

Slipping his attention to Stone's groin, Valentine took in

the bulge behind the man's fly. "So." His smile turned lascivious as he eased to his knees. "If I were to come over there, you'd let me open your pants and suck on your meat?"

As odd and out of the blue as his proposition seemed to be, the idea of tasting Stone's flesh made his mouth water, and Valentine would be more than happy to take advantage of his mate's need.

"Yeah," Stone let out on a breathy huff. "Yeah, I'd totally let you do that."

"Perfect," Valentine rumbled.

Rocking forward, Valentine reached for Stone. As his mate watched him with intense blue eyes, arousal swimming within their depths — mixed a little with wariness — Valentine vowed to erase every other past lover's mouth from his human's mind . . . or at least surpass their memories.

CHAPTER EIGHT

Stone knew he was thinking with his dick, but he'd been sitting there waiting for Valentine to proposition him in some way. He'd begun to anticipate it. His dick had even grown hard from his thoughts.

Except, it had never come. Instead, Valentine had acted like the perfect gentleman . . . mostly. He'd touched Stone innocently from time to time, but that had only enflamed his unexpected arousal.

Having no desire to hike back with a hard-on, and feeling quite relaxed from the couple of beers he'd drank, Stone had decided to make the first move. To his pleasure, Valentine had quickly responded. The man appeared more than happy to take Stone up on his not-so-subtle request for a blowjob.

Stone watched Valentine crawl toward him, looking very much like a predator on three legs. He watched Valentine settle on his left elbow, keeping his weight off his casted arm. When the other man reached for his fly with his right hand, Stone couldn't help but tense a little, regardless of the fact that he'd instigated this.

"Just relax, my mate," Valentine rumbled huskily, his tone full of promise. "I'm going to make you feel so damn good."

"O-Okay." Stone hated the hint of uncertainty in his voice. He hadn't had anyone else touch his dick in months, and he wanted this. Instilling a demand into his voice, he ordered, "Take care of me, Val."

Valentine chuckled, the sound deep and low. "Oh, I will,

Stone," he assured, gripping the fly of Stone's jeans and expertly popping open the button. "Such good care of you."

Even one-handed, Valentine made quick work of Stone's fly. With the zipper down, his erection pressed between the flaps, clearly defined, even beneath the fabric of his briefs. When Valentine hummed appreciatively and skimmed the tips of his nails up his length, tingles erupted through Stone's groin, his shaft twitching. Heat swirled in his gut, and he sucked in a sharp breath.

Giving him a heated smirk, Valentine eased his fingertips into the waistband of his underwear. He teased his forefingers over Stone's hidden crown, massaging his swollen head. The move yanked a groan from Stone's throat as his cock throbbed, and the light stimulation sent jolts of pleasure down his stalk.

"Gods, the sounds you make," Valentine growled, arousal filling his tone. "Love them. Can't wait to hear more." Then he lifted Stone's underwear up and over his shaft and ordered, "Lift your hips."

Panting harshly, it was Stone's turn to obey. He arched his back, planting his feet, and lifted his ass off the blanket. Seeing Valentine's one-handed struggle, Stone rested his weight on his left forearm and used his right to help the other man.

Once Valentine had Stone's jeans and underwear halfway down his thighs, he moved his hand to Stone's hip and urged him to relax back onto the blanket. His cock bobbed from his groin as Stone watched Valentine lean closer. When his soon-to-be lover—*god, does letting him blow me make Val my lover*—blew warm breath across his crown, Stone moaned as his prick twitched, a bead of pre-cum oozing from his slit.

When Valentine stuck out his tongue and swept it around his crown, Stone groaned and vowed to worry about it all later. The hot wet appendage caused a shudder to work through his gut. His cock throbbed with his need.

Stone felt damn tempted to beg . . . or demand . . . when Valentine swiped his tongue up his stalk from root to tip. To his relief, as soon as he reached the crown again, Valentine opened his mouth and wrapped his lips around his knob. Stone groaned appreciatively as the other man sucked lightly on his swollen crown. It almost felt as if he was nursing on him, searching for more pre-cum, and Stone's body was helpless but to give it to him.

With a moan of pleasure, Stone flopped back onto the blanket, sprawling. He gripped the fabric beneath him, his cock throbbing and twitching within the sweet confines of Valentine's hot mouth. His pre-cum flowed as his balls grew heavy with his impending release.

Stone's head began to swim, and he shuddered. Bucking his hips, he searched for more. Instead of stopping the move, Valentine went with it, accepting his cock deeper into his mouth. The wet heat enveloping his entire length felt beyond exquisite, yanking a barking cry from his throat that he didn't ever recall making before.

As much as Stone wanted to hold the position, his stomach muscles ached, and he had to relax back down. To his delight, Valentine followed him, only allowing him to slip halfway out before taking him deep again. Stone moaned again as Valentine began sucking and bobbing on his cock, using his tongue and lips to stimulate in a way he felt certain he'd never before experienced.

When Valentine cradled Stone's balls, he felt his eyes begin to roll back. His testicles started to tighten, and tingles erupted at the base of his spine, heralding that the end was near. The fingertip massaging behind his heavy sack was the last straw.

Crying Valentine's name, Stone came hard. His orgasm rocked through his system, making spots dance across his vision. His senses sang as Valentine continued to work him, causing the sensations to go on and on. His mind floated in euphoric bliss, his body trembling.

Finally, the stimulation became too much, and Stone moaned and shivered for a new reason. To his relief, the other man understood and released his prick. The sudden cooler air caused goose bumps to rise on his thighs, and Stone sighed deeply, feeling beyond fantastic.

A familiar *slap, slap* sound registered, and Stone peeled open eyelids he didn't even remember closing. It took a couple of blinks before he could focus. Seeing Valentine levered partly over him, his features etched with bliss as he stared intently at him, wasn't what caused Stone's body to flush with a fresh wave of heat. Instead, it was the fact that Valentine held his thick, dark erection in his hand and was beating off. He pointed the tip of his swollen shaft toward Stone's groin, his thick crown nearly touching Stone's still half-hard dick.

Snapping his attention back to Valentine's face, Stone sucked in a sharp breath upon seeing the feral expression there. For just a second, he felt certain he spotted something wild, primitive, swimming within the depths of his eyes. Then it was gone as Valentine came, roaring Stone's name.

Feeling the hot splash of Valentine's cum hit the flesh of his stomach and groin yanked a surprised gasp from Stone. He snapped his attention from the blissfully pained expression on Valentine's face as he came to where the man sprayed his seed over him. Panting, Stone watched as the large man's erection stopped pulsing, a final drip oozing from the slit to land on his balls, sending tingles through him.

Stone lifted his gaze to Valentine's face, and a gasp escaped his throat. His new lover peered at him with an intense expression. When Valentine swept his gaze over Stone's body, a satisfied smile curved his full lips.

Then Valentine moved a hand to Stone's body and began working the semen into his flesh, and it suddenly hit Stone.

"You're marking me," Stone blurted.

Valentine flicked his gaze up to meet Stone's eyes. "Yeah." He didn't sound the least bit shy or reticent about it. Instead, he sounded oh-so-very satisfied.

Before Stone could come up with how he felt about that, or even a response, Valentine lowered his head and sealed his mouth over Stone's. An instant later, he found himself with a mouthful of Valentine's tongue. For a second, Stone froze, shocked by the brazen move.

Then Stone's own flavor mixed with Valentine's deep masculine one registered, and he found he loved it. It suddenly didn't matter that he was kissing a man because said man tasted damn fantastic. Returning the kiss, Stone allowed himself to get swept away as a fresh wave of arousal heated him from the inside out.

*

Just three days before, if someone would've told Stone that he would openly be on a date with a man, he would have laughed in their face.

Or I would have told them to fuck off.

Except, there Stone was, sitting at a table in *Caribou's*—Stone Ridge's steak house and favorite dating hot spot—enjoying an evening meal with Valentine. He cut into his steak, enjoying the succulent meat that was grilled medium rare to perfection. His mashed potatoes and gravy melted in his mouth. Even the lobster mac and cheese was better than anything he'd ever enjoyed.

Of course, Stone supposed part of it could have been a combination of him being sexually sated combined with a little fatigue from a long day at work. He knew Valentine didn't work, and he had no idea what the man did with the majority of his days, but that didn't mean that he could shirk off. Stone had bills to pay.

That did mean Valentine would show up at his door shortly after Stone texted him that he was home.

After that first date, Stone had spent every evening with the man. He'd enjoyed their make-out session from their first date so much that it had ended in a frotting session that gave him a second almost as epic release as the blowjob. They'd finished up by lying with each other, dirty and messy, talking about little things for a while. When the seed had turned uncomfortable, Stone had given in and gone skinny dipping with Valentine to wash up.

Even after sharing a couple of orgasms with the man, Stone still hadn't been ready to embrace in the water, and he appreciated Valentine's understanding, so they'd kept it to a brief, utilitarian clean-up. Stone hadn't missed the appreciative heated looks the other man had given him, though.

The next night, Valentine had taken him to a large A-frame home positioned behind an even more massive farm-style home deep in the woods. He'd introduced him to the rest of the guys. They'd all been friendly and welcoming. They'd grilled burgers and hotdogs. After the meal, Valentine had come through on his promise and taught Stone *Dutch Blitz*.

Stone couldn't remember the last time he'd had so much fun playing cards. The game was fast-paced, and the guys were truly cutthroat. At times, Stone had struggled to even keep up with their movements, they were so speedy.

The prior evening, they'd stayed in at Stone's place. He'd ordered a pizza from *Spieron's Bar and Grill*, picking it up on his way home from work. The police in the area were used to seeing his big rig parked on the side of the road and never gave him any trouble.

After digesting from their meal, Stone had shown Valentine the rope and obstacle course he'd mentioned. As it turned out, his big lover had been far more agile than he would have imagined. He'd been slow and wobbled a few times here and there, but he'd managed to make it through without falling too many times.

The evenings were intense, leaving Stone sated and exhausted. Valentine was an insatiable and creative lover. He used his lips, teeth, hands, and tongue on Stone's body in ways that left him writhing. While Stone hadn't sucked Valentine's dick, he had gotten over his reticence to touch the other man's cock, and he'd even tasted his lover's seed. Stone had been surprised to find the slightly salty cream had a pretty tasty flavor.

"I'm off work tomorrow," Stone told Valentine, trying to decide how to broach the subject that had been plaguing him. He hoped to spend the day in bed exploring his lover. Valentine had done it to him plenty of times, and Stone wanted to figure out how to return certain favors. "I was wondering—"

"Percy Stonewall?"

Narrowing his eyes upon hearing his detested first name—*what the hell was my sweet mother thinking*—Stone lifted his gaze to find a man in a suit standing beside their table. "Yes," he hissed through clenched teeth.

The man placed a brown manila envelope on the table. "You've been served, sir." Then the man turned and walked away.

"Served?" Valentine sounded just as confused as Stone felt. "What's that mean?"

Frowning while shaking his head, Stone picked up the envelope. He shook out the papers. After moving his nearly empty plate aside, he spread them on the table and took in the official-looking documents.

The more Stone read, the faster his heart thudded in his chest. His mouth dried out, and he grabbed his beer bottle, chugging the rest before plunking it back onto the table. Disbelief flooded him as he reread certain key paragraphs.

Feeling Valentine's hand over his own yanked Stone out of

his shock. He jerked his head up and stared at the other man, his mind reeling.

"Hey." Valentine squeezed his fingers. "What's wrong?" His expression turned earnest. "Whatever it is, I promise I'll help fix it."

Stone didn't know how Valentine could promise that. Hell, if the information in the documents was true, he doubted the man would even stick around. That thought sent a shocking stab of sadness through his heart, and he realized he was going to miss Valentine . . . so very badly.

Shit. Did I fall in love with this guy in three days? How the hell did that happen?

Valentine squeezed his hand again. "Talk to me, Stone."

Knowing he had to get it over with, Stone tapped the papers. "According to this, I have a daughter." He watched Valentine's eyes widen, and he knew he needed to get the rest out there. "A woman named Melissa Smithson is suing me for back child support, as well as demanding the court set up regular ongoing payments."

As Stone had feared, Valentine straightened, pulling his hand away as shock took over his dark-featured expression.

A stab of pain hit Stone right in the chest, and he just knew he'd just lost something precious.

CHAPTER NINE

Valentine straightened, shock rolling through him upon hearing that news.

My mate has a kid? A daughter? How come he never said anything? Maybe he just needed more time before revealing something like that? Kids are a huge thing when it comes to new relationships.

Still, the distrust hurt.

Then Valentine took in Stone's expression—hurt mixed with resignation.

Oh, damn. He thinks I'm going to walk away because of this.

So not happening.

Clearing his throat, Valentine rested his forearms back on the table and took Stone's hand again. He felt the stiffness there and massaged his mate's palm lightly. Valentine forced a small smile as he waited for Stone to meet his gaze.

"So, a daughter," Valentine stated once Stone was looking him in the eye. "That's . . . unexpected. How old is she? What's her name?"

Stone blinked once before his brows furrowed. "I don't know."

Valentine scented Stone's honesty, and what he'd said earlier suddenly registered. "According to that paper," he whispered, repeating his mate's words. Staring intently at Stone, he asked, "You didn't know you have a daughter?"

Shaking his head while still sporting an expression that Valentine was coming to recognize as shell-shocked, Stone mumbled, "No woman has ever contacted me about knocking her up."

"Then how the hell can they claim she's yours?" Valentine wondered out loud.

Obviously not having an answer, Stone just shrugged.

"Then we need to find out," Valentine declared, realizing he needed help. "I'll get the check." He squeezed Stone's hand again. "We'll figure this out."

When Valentine went to draw away, Stone tightened his grip. "You're not dumping me?"

Valentine smiled warmly at his mate. "Oh, no, my mate. You're stuck with me." Then he rose and rounded to Stone's side of the booth. Ignoring those around him, Valentine bent and pecked a quick kiss to his human's lips. "Be right back."

As Valentine strode away from the table in search of their waiter, he could practically feel Stone's gaze on him. He quickly located someone to get their check and returned to the table. They boxed up the rest of their meals, paid for them, and headed outside.

"While we drive, I'm going to make a couple of calls," Valentine explained as he placed his helmet on his head. "I think I know someone who can help us." After a second of hesitation, Valentine amended, "Or, at least, has the connections to help us."

Stone nodded, his brows furrowing. "Uh, why are you taking responsibility for this?" Cocking his head, he pointed out, "This is my problem."

Valentine touched Stone's jaw, enjoying the feel of his mate's clean-shaven skin. "Because we're a couple," he declared, not caring that it had only been a few days. "And couples work through problems together." After a second of hesitation, Valentine asked, "Unless you already have a lawyer to look into shit like this?"

After opening his mouth, then closing it just as quickly, Stone shook his head. "No, I don't," he admitted, twisting his lips ruefully.

"Okay then." Valentine dipped his head and pecked a kiss to his cheek below the side of the helmet. "Then let me help with this, because I know I can."

Valentine watched Stone nod, and satisfaction filled him. His bear liked that his mate was accepting his assistance. Over the last few days, Valentine had done his best to curb his shifter nature to care for and provide for his mate, but he knew he wouldn't be able to in this instance. His need was pushing forward, fast and intense. Valentine needed to help Stone. Considering the way he was going to go about doing it, he knew it would be explanation time soon enough.

Guess it'll be good that we'll be at Alpha Declan's place. At least, I hope he'll be available.

With that thought in mind, Valentine used the *Bluetooth* in his helmet to call Congo. He explained the situation as he understood it, then asked his alpha's permission to contact Alpha Declan. While the wolf shifter didn't stand much on ceremony, he didn't just want to show up at his house without permission from either of them.

"I'll talk to Declan and smooth the way," Congo assured him. "Not that I think it'll take much convincing."

"Thank you, Congo." Valentine hung up and smiled at Stone as he switched channels on his radio so he could talk to his mate. "Follow me."

Stone nodded. While his expression appeared curious, he didn't ask.

Valentine led the way deeper into the mountains and along the winding roads. He didn't try to fill the silence as he had no idea what to say. Valentine couldn't imagine being in Stone's situation, finding out via the courts that he had a daughter he didn't know about.

I wonder what she's like. How old is she? How long has the mother been caring for her alone? Did she try to find Stone earlier? Or is she only after money? Will Stone want to try to be part of her life? Where are they located?

Those questions and a million more flashed through Valentine's brain. He couldn't wait to get the answers.

Whatever happens, Stone is going to learn that I'll be right by his side. He's my mate.

Hell, Valentine knew that his entire sleuth would be behind Stone. Probably the wolf pack, too. While Valentine didn't think Congo had confirmed with Alpha Declan about staying in the area after Kontra had moved on, he knew the offer had been made. The sleuth intended to take him up on it.

Well, most of us.

Valentine would miss Shannon, but the bear's place was with his mate, Evan. At that time, the blossoming warlock needed guidance and instruction, and that could only come from Draven and Tim. When Kontra and his gang left in the next few weeks, Shannon and Evan would be with them.

Valentine turned his motorcycle into Declan's driveway, appreciating the paved lane. He'd overheard tales of when it had been a badly potholed gravel track. They'd cleaned it up since then.

Parking in front of a large, detached garage, Valentine shut off his engine. He swung off, pleased to see Stone doing the same without hesitation. Valentine hung his helmet on one handlebar before crossing to his mate and resting a hand on his lower back.

Stone arched a brow, but Valentine just smiled as he urged him toward the front door.

"Where are we?" Stone asked softly, looking up at the gorgeous lodge. The place had been expanded over the years, and the stone façade went halfway up the walls of the first floor. The rest was beautiful wooden beams with metal accents. "A lawyer's place?"

Valentine could imagine why Stone would guess that. The place screamed money. Of course, when you lived several centuries, accumulating wealth was easy enough if you had any business sense, which many people in the wolf pack did.

"No, this is the home of Alpha Declan McIntire," Valentine explained to his mate, deciding it was time to lay it all out on the line. "You know him as the area's head park ranger." They'd reached the top of the steps, and Valentine urged Stone to pause and turn to face him. He could see the door opening out of the corner of his eye as he held his mate's gaze and explained, "I know Declan as the leader of the wolf shifter pack that controls the territory in and around Stone Ridge."

Stone blinked once before narrowing his eyes and tipping his head just a little. "I'm sorry. Did you just say . . . wolf shifter pack?" He looked at him askance. "What the hell is that?"

"It's just how it sounds," Declan cut in, stepping out of the house. He held out his hand. "I'm Declan McIntire, alpha of the Stone Ridge wolf pack."

For an instant, Stone hesitated, and Valentine would bet that only good manners caused him to reach out and accept the wolf shifter's hand.

"Uh, nice to meet you," Stone responded, still obviously wary. He glanced between them as he lowered his hand back to his side. "What the hell is going on?"

"Come in," Declan beckoned, crooking his fingers. "We'll explain everything."

Valentine returned his hand to Stone's back and guided him inside. While he could feel the tension in his mate's back, his human went. His shoulders were rigid, and he peered around furtively, as if his military training was kicking in and he was searching for exits.

Wishing to soothe Stone, Valentine slid his hand up and down his spine. "I know this is going to sound fantastic and crazy, but I swear it's all true."

"Ah, that dreaded phrase," a dry voice sounded from near the hallway. A lean, tawny-haired man leaned against the wall with his arms crossed over his chest and a smirk curving his lips. His hazel eyes twinkled with mischief. "Explaining shifters and other paranormals to humans always sounds ridiculous." He straightened from the wall. "I've been right where you are, Stone," he claimed. "I'm Jared or Prier. I answer to both." He waved his hand dismissively. "Anyway, I have some information on that Melissa Smithson yahoo who's suing you."

Well, at least that was some good news.

Then Jared waggled his brows before winking at Stone. "Welcome to the rabbit hole, Alice."

Rolling his eyes, Declan muttered under his breath, "May the gods give me strength." Then he frowned at Jared and stated, "Please tell me Kajika will be here soon to keep you and yer mouth in line."

"Eh, in maybe an hour or so," Jared replied glibly. "Until then, I get to tell Stone all about the fantastic perks of being mated to a shifter." His expression turned lascivious as he continued, "And let me tell you, the sexual gratification is beyond belief."

Declan groaned.

Stone gaped at Jared for a few seconds before turning to look at those around him. "What the hell, Val?"

Valentine urged Stone into the study Declan and Jared had been leading them to. "Take a seat, handsome," he urged, moving toward a loveseat. "This is going to take a little time to explain."

To Valentine's relief, Stone sat, even if he did remain perched on the edge of the cushion. Settling next to his mate, he wrapped his arms around him. A moment later, Declan's mate, Lark, joined them, and the explanations began.

CHAPTER TEN

Stone wondered if a person's head could explode from too much information.

Probably not.

Lifting up a hand, Stone requested, "Okay. Please, stop."

The man who'd been introduced as the alpha's mate, Lark, fell silent, a worried look creasing his cute blond features.

"Thank you," Stone murmured, issuing a sigh of relief. After glancing at those filling the study—Congo and Zion had joined them at one point, as well as Jared's lover, partner, mate, whatever, Kajika—he did his best to ignore the variety of concerned expressions. Forcing his tone to come out even, Stone claimed, "I can only process one thing at a time right now, and the existence of shifters isn't it." When Valentine squeezed his hand and opened his mouth, he quickly cut in, "We'll talk about your claim about us being mates later. I promise. I just"—he pointed at his summons papers spread out on the coffee table—"I need to deal with this daughter situation first. Can we? Please?"

Stone would forever deny the slightest hint of begging in his tone.

Yep. I'm a little overwhelmed.

"Sure, Stone." An understanding smile curved Valentine's full lips as he squeezed Stone's hand. "I understand." After a glance around, he smiled at Stone again. "This is a lot. I know it is. Our time will come later."

Nodding, Stone found himself silently agreeing. After everything he'd heard, he knew he wouldn't just be able to walk away. Not to mention, when Stone had been in the restaurant and worried about Valentine leaving him, his chest had felt as if it was impossible to breathe.

At least the bear I hit with my semi is fine.

That had been a hell of a shock—Valentine had been that bear. He hadn't wanted to believe it until Kajika had transformed into a wolf right there in the study. Only Valentine's hands on him, holding him and soothing him, had kept Stone from losing his shit.

"Okay, so, this claim that I have a daughter." Stone focused on Jared. "When I first walked in, you said you had information on that. On this Melissa person?"

Jared nodded once, his voice turning serious. "Melissa Smithson lives in Denver," he told him. "She's what's known as a military groupie. Maybe it's a *Daddy* thing. Her father's a general." Grimacing, Jared explained, "If you went to a club in Denver with your tags on"—he pointed to the dog tags Stone pretty much always still wore—"then Melissa would've been all over you." Arching a brow, he added, "And her friends call her Missy."

The image of a sultry brunette entered Stone's mind, and he grimaced. "Oh, god." He rubbed a hand over his face.

"Remember her now?" Jared asked with a wry smile.

"Yeah," Stone admitted. "That had to have been . . ." He shook his head slowly, racking his brain for a timeframe.

"Around eighteen months ago," Jared supplied for him. "She gave birth to a girl, Laticia, which she's calling Letty." Turning around his laptop, he pointed. "Social media posts."

Stone found his gaze riveted on the screen. There in Melissa's arms was a baby with a pink headband around her brow. The chubby, red-faced infant looked about ready to let out a wail, but Stone still found her enchanting.

The little girl also had his vivid blue eyes. An eye color he'd shared with his mother.

"Damn," Valentine whispered from next to him. "She's

adorable." Then, to Stone's shock, his lover looked at Jared and asked, "How do we get custody?"

Stone snapped his focus away from the picture to Valentine. "What?"

Seeing the slight pink that managed to stain his lover's dark skin and how he hunched his shoulders and ducked his head, Stone felt his heart squeeze for a new reason.

Damn. How could I not love this guy? Fast sure, but sometimes that happens . . . even with the human half . . .

Or so he'd been told.

"You want to get custody of my daughter?"

Valentine shrugged one shoulder, looking shy. "I've always wanted kids."

While Stone had thought about it a time or two, it'd been before his mother passed that he'd given it any serious thought. For some reason, however, the thought of raising a child with Valentine held a lot of appeal. Turning his attention back to the babe on the screen, Letty, and seeing his mother's blue eyes staring back at him, there was no way that Stone couldn't at least try.

"Is there a chance of that?" Stone asked slowly, focusing back on Jared. The tech guy seemed to be the one in the know. "For us to get custody?"

"Are you sure you want that?" Valentine murmured, leaning close. "I don't want you to try to do something just because of me."

It was Stone's turn to squeeze Valentine's hand to reassure him. "You see those pretty blue eyes on that little baby?" he asked. Once his big black lover nodded, Stone shared, "Those are my mother's eyes. If we don't adopt her, how are we supposed to tell her about her grandmother Iris and her great-grandmother Sarah?"

Stone's heart rate sped up just at the idea of sharing stories of his mother and grandmother with his daughter. Both women had been strong, fierce, and loving. They'd given him unconditional love and the drive to succeed.

"I'd sure love to share them with little Letty," Stone admitted with a warm smile. "I think trying to get custody is a fantastic idea."

Valentine grinned back, his expression somehow full of relief and anticipation all at the same time.

"I think there's definitely a chance," Jared chimed in. When Stone focused on the man, his expression turned just a little malicious. "Her general father is the one who used his military channels to figure out who the girl's father is. I'm pretty sure searching private medical files is illegal." Chuckling darkly, Jared continued, "And he's also buried records of some rather unsavory activities his daughter's been involved in. I think we can sway a court judge to rule in a loving, stable gay couple's favor."

"There's something more to your animosity," Stone guessed, reading the man's expression. "What's going on?" He was a little afraid to ask what kind of unsavory activities Melissa might have been involved in, but he had to ask. "Is Letty healthy?"

Jared seemed to understand perfectly, and he nodded quickly. "Yeah. Although I don't like the general because he's a bigoted asshole who gets his kids out of taking responsibility for their shit, he kept her clean during her pregnancy." With a grimace, Jared went on to say, "Right now, Letty lives with her grandfather, so at least she's safe. It also puts another hole in Melissa's suit to get child support."

Nodding slowly, Stone thought about how quickly his life was about to change, and not just because of the paranormal aspect. Raising a child was expensive and time-consuming. He would need to remodel or expand, and that would cost money.

Wait, that's not the only thing that costs money.

"I can't afford an attorney," Stone blurted out, worry filling him. As soon as Valentine opened his mouth, he guessed what the man was about to offer. "And you're not paying for it, damn it."

"Neither of ye is paying for it," Declan stated, his accented voice cutting into the conversation. Stone bet there was a story about how the Irish-born wolf shifter had ended up in the states, but Stone would probably never have the courage to ask. Declan pinned a tight smile on Stone and told him, "Ye're in the paranormal world now, Stone. Ye live here in me territory with yer shifter mate." His gray-eyed gaze swept over Valentine before refocusing on Stone. "That means what effects ye is pack business. Ye're being sued. The pack will help handle it." Lifting a hand to stall Stone's reply when he opened his mouth, not that Stone knew what he was going to say, the black wolf alpha told him, "I've already put in a call to our pack lawyer, Clancy. Ye'll meet him in a day or two after he consults with Jared. In the meantime, I think ye should focus on sorting out yer bond. We'll touch base with ye about yer lawsuit when we have more information or need more of the same from ye."

For some reason, Stone felt as if his problem had just been taken over, and he'd been dismissed.

Considering Valentine was rising to his feet, saying, "Thank you, Alpha Declan. We appreciate it," Stone figured he was right. Valentine gripped his upper arm and squeezed, urging Stone to his feet. "Come on, handsome. Let's go somewhere private to talk."

Stone knew what conversation was coming next, and he nodded as he rose. "Can we head to my place?" he asked, needing the comfort of familiarity.

"Yeah." Valentine offered him a reassuring smile. "Let's get out of here." With an eyebrow waggle, he added, "We still have that chocolate lava cake to enjoy. I changed it a *to go* order when we left so suddenly."

Even though Stone wasn't certain he could manage to eat

the tasty treat anytime soon, he still chuckled and nodded.

"I'll talk to you before too long, Val," Congo called behind them. After Valentine had issued a confirmation, Stone heard Congo say, "I suppose you know that I'd like to petition that most of my sleuth stay on the outskirts of your territory, Alpha Declan."

Stone missed the wolf shifter's response as they headed out the front door. A moment later, they were back on their motorcycles and driving to his cabin. Occasionally, Stone glanced Valentine's way, taking in his pensive expression.

The need to set his lover at ease urged Stone to drive a little bit faster.

*

Once they reached Stone's cabin, he opened his small garage and wheeled his motorcycle inside. He peered over his shoulder and spotted Valentine standing awkwardly beside his own bike. Taking in the usually confident man's bearing, Stone bit back a smile at how cute he looked.

Not something I should ever call him. I know.

"Park your motorcycle inside," Stone encouraged, indicating the empty space beside his own. "It's supposed to rain tonight."

Valentine gaped at him for a second before he started hurrying forward, and Stone knew his lover had gotten the message. Stone didn't have to work the next day, and he didn't plan for the other man to leave. They had plenty to talk about, and he still wanted to implement his plan of exploring his lover's big body while naked.

As Stone had driven home, he'd realized that the fact that Valentine was a bear shifter hadn't changed anything in Stone's mind. Why would it? He loved the guy, even if he knew he wouldn't be able to express himself for some time.

I am a guy, after all.

Once Stone had led the way into his cabin, he headed to the kitchen and grabbed them both bottles of water. He saw the way Valentine stood near the counter, watching him intently. Stone saw the hunger in his lover's eyes, and a fissure of arousal surged through his body. His blood flowed south, and his dick plumped behind the fly of his jeans, just as it always did.

Yeah, I can totally get used to this.

Valentine's nostrils flared, telling Stone that the man had scented his arousal. That was something else that would take some getting used to. Shifters could smell certain things, from lies to arousal to anger to fear and everything in between.

Enough thinking of that.

"So." Stone smiled and swept what he hoped was a hungry look over Valentine. "I think we should go to my bedroom, get naked, and you should bite me."

Never in a million years would Stone think he would utter such words, but there it was. He knew that was part of bonding, and he wanted that with Valentine. He wanted Valentine to know that Stone was all in.

"If I do that, there's no going back, Stone."

Smirking upon hearing Valentine's warning, Stone countered, "There's already no going back, Val." He grinned and shrugged. "You're mine. I'm yours." Stone sauntered past a surprised-looking Valentine and headed toward his bedroom door. "The bite is just a formality."

"Not to a shifter," Valentine countered, stalking after him. "It's an imperative."

"Then you better come do it, Val," Stone taunted, backing into his bedroom. Giving his lover a lascivious once-over, he pulled his undershirt and flannel over his head and dropped them onto the floor. "You want to . . . right here." Stone tipped his chin up and to the side, exaggerating the tendon of his neck enticingly.

Valentine growled and groaned all in one sound. "Fuck,

Stone."

By the time Valentine had whipped his polo shirt awkwardly over his head — slightly hindered by the cast — and dropped it to the floor, Stone was naked and on the bed. He had his legs slightly apart in as brazen a move as he could muster, and his hands were crossed behind his head. Even as nerves skittered through him, eagerness caused his prick to bob at his groin.

The whine that escaped Valentine was pretty damn gratifying, ramping up Stone's need. He watched his lover shove off his boots, socks, and jeans. The fact that Valentine didn't bother with underwear made a lot more sense to him now.

As Valentine rested one knee on the bed, he asked, "Are you sure?"

Knowing he needed to be honest, Stone admitted, "I'm still not ready for fucking, but yes, I want your bite." He offered his lover a reassuring smile and told him, "I'm sure we'll get there, but I know you need to bite to help your bear settle, and I'm more than happy to give you both that."

Valentine nodded as he prowled forward. "Consider this, my mate," he stated softly as he drew closer. "A female shifter will give her human mate a claiming bite, but she can't very well spill semen into him."

The odd comment derailed Stone's thoughts, and he tried to process whatever Valentine was trying to tell him. "Uh, what are you trying to say?"

"A human male would go down on a female, ingesting her natural lubricant." Valentine's cheeks darkened just a smidge, betraying his embarrassment at discussing such things. "It takes a little longer for the bond to take place, but it does happen."

What Valentine was explaining clicked, and Stone grinned. "So, you bite me, and I drink your semen," he verbalized his understanding. "It'll take longer, but it'll happen while I'm wrapping my brain around the idea of anal sex."

Valentine nodded once, his expression turning feral as he eyed Stone's neck. "Yessss," he hissed.

"I'm all in," Stone declared, tipping his head back.

His lover pounced, and Stone gasped as he watched the bear shifter's canines lengthen. As his shifter sank those large teeth into his neck, Stone had just an instant to second-guess himself—those teeth looked huge, after all.

Then the pleasure crashed through him as Valentine suckled at his neck, drinking Stone's blood.

No, not pleasure.

Bliss.

Ecstasy.

Heaven.

As Stone rode wave after wave of indescribable sensations, he cried Val's name as one thought reverberated through his brain.

Oh, yeah. This was a perfect idea.

Change was coming, but Stone could handle anything because Valentine would be right beside him.

ABOUT THE AUTHOR

Charlie started writing fantasy when she was eight, and after stumbling onto her first erotic romance at age nineteen, she realized her true calling. She now focuses on writing gay erotic romance, normally of the paranormal variety, with heroes of all kinds. With the help and support of her husband, Charlie finally fulfilled one of her life-long goals . . . move to acreage with her horses. You can often find her curled up with her laptop and a cup of tea or glass of wine, creating her next adventure. Charlie enjoys exploring the mountains of her new Oregon home on horseback, 4-wheeler, or motorcycle.

She can be reached at ch.richards2010@yahoo.com

Or visit her at www.charlie-richards.com.

www.ingramcontent.com/pod-product-compliance
Lightning Source LLC
Chambersburg PA
CBHW071628140626
46555CB00021B/1502